Samuel French Acting E

Skintight

by Joshua Harmon

FOR PRODUCTION INQUIRIES

UNITED STATES AND CANADA
info@concordtheatricals.com
1-866-979-0447

UNITED KINGDOM AND EUROPE
licensing@concordtheatricals.co.uk
020-7054-7200

Each title is subject to availability from Concord Theatricals Corp., depending upon country of performance. Please be aware that *SKINTIGHT* may not be licensed by Concord Theatricals Corp. in your territory. Professional and amateur producers should contact the nearest Concord Theatricals Corp. office or licensing partner to verify availability.

MUSIC AND THIRD-PARTY MATERIALS USE NOTE

IMPORTANT BILLING AND CREDIT REQUIREMENTS

SKINTIGHT premiered on June 21, 2018 at the Roundabout Theatre Company's Laura Pels Theatre in New York City. The production was directed by Daniel Aukin, with set design by Lauren Helpern, costume design by Jess Goldstein, lighting design by Pat Collins, and sound design and original compositions by Eric Shimelonis. The production stage manager was Jill Cordle. The cast was as follows:

JODI ISAAC	Idina Menzel
ELLIOT ISAAC	Jack Wetherall
BENJAMIN CULLEN	Eli Gelb
TREY	Will Brittain
ORSOLYA	Cynthia Mace
JEFF	Stephen Carrasco

SKINTIGHT transferred to the Geffen Playhouse and premiered on September 13, 2019. The production was directed by Daniel Aukin, with set design by Lauren Helpern, costume design by China Lee, lighting design by Pat Collins, and sound design by Vincent Oliveri. The production stage manager was Ross Jackson. The cast was as follows:

JODI ISAAC	Idina Menzel
ELLIOT ISAAC	Harry Groener
BENJAMIN CULLEN	Eli Gelb
TREY	Will Brittain
ORSOLYA	Kimberly Jürgen
JEFF	Jeff Skowron

CHARACTERS

JODI ISAAC – mid-forties

ELLIOT ISAAC – (almost) seventy, Jodi's father

BENJAMIN CULLEN – twenty, Jodi's son

TREY – twenty, Elliot's partner

ORSOLYA – fifties/sixties, a female housekeeper

JEFF – forties, a male houseboy

SETTING

A West Village townhouse on Horatio Street.

The kind you stand outside when you're walking those incredible streets in the Village and dream of entering.

Well, now we're inside.

The immaculate, pristine, pitch-perfect living room of Elliot Isaac.

A couch in the center. The kind of incredibly stiff couch that is aesthetically pleasing, but not at all what you want to curl up on, under a blanket, when you're sad, which is really what most of the people in this play want to do.

A staircase at the back leads to the second floor.

ACT I

Scene One

(Morning. October.)

(Lights up on **ELLIOT ISAAC**, *standing at the bottom of his staircase.* **JODI ISAAC** *stands near him, having just entered.)*

ELLIOT. What are you doing here?

JODI. I thought I'd surprise you.

ELLIOT. Why?

JODI. It's your birthday tomorrow?

ELLIOT. So?

JODI. So, I thought you might like to see me.

ELLIOT. But I don't want to do anything for my birthday. I told you – I was explicitly... explicit.

JODI. I just took a red-eye, to be here.

ELLIOT. I didn't ask you to take a red-eye –

JODI. No you didn't ask me to, but I was trying to be –

ELLIOT. And I hate surprises –

JODI. I was trying to do something nice for –

ELLIOT. I turned down three different invitations because I don't want –

JODI. Can you just be excited to see me? Ok? Right now, I need *someone* to be excited to see me when I walk in a room. I need *that*, right now, at least...

I know you hate surprises, I just... needed...

(She hugs her dad. She's upset. Then deeply upset, burying her face into his chest. He holds her, his frustration subsiding.)

7

JODI. Sorry. Sorry. I'm just...

> *(Quick beat.)*

ELLIOT. What's going on?

JODI. Nothing. Nothing. I don't know.

> *(Beat.)*

Greg, had his engagement party last night.

ELLIOT. Ohhhh.

JODI. Yeah. Oh. Exactly. Oh. At OUR favorite restaurant

ELLIOT. At –

JODI. Yeah. And he apparently invited all our friends? Like, every single one, most of who, I mean, those are MY friends, because *Greg* could never be BOTHERED to put in the TIME to actually stay in touch with ANYONE, but there they were, MY friends, with MY kids, at MY favorite restaurant, and I just, like couldn't physically be in LA knowing that was happening.

ELLIOT. So you came here. That's –

JODI. Like, my friends are smart, ok? These are intelligent – Bill Rosen used to work at NASA, ok? And Rochelle, I'm pretty sure Rochelle is in MENSA – I'm not positive, but like, she was on *JEOPARDY*. My friends are not idiots, but last night they stood around toasting Greg like this is even real and – did I tell you how old the little spinner is?

ELLIOT. Spinner?

JODI. She does that, you know, that cycling, spinning, SoulCycle shit.

ELLIOT. Ok...

JODI. She's twenty-*four*.

ELLIOT. Ok.

JODI. Greg is fifty, Daddy.

ELLIOT. Right.

JODI. *Fifty*. And Misty is twenty-four.

ELLIOT. Misty?

JODI. I mean, this is a grown man, a grown up grown up man, father of two boys, one of whom is TWENTY, I might add, which is, I might add, just four years younger than, than than – I did the math. Ok? I *did* the math, and when I met Greg, when we first got together, the little spinner who broke up my marriage? Was one.

When Greg and I went to Antigua – remember when we went to Antigua, so early on but it was an impulse – at that resort, you know, the one where you did that campaign, where the models were swimming naked in the ocean, but left their jeans all bunched up in the sand, you remember that campaign?

ELLIOT. Surrender.

JODI. While Greg and I were at that resort, like, not to be graphic, Daddy, but while we were having like the best sex of our lives, our ADULT lives, this *person* was getting her diaper changed, because she didn't yet possess the motor skills to WIPE HER OWN ASS. When this *child* started eating solid foods, Greg was busy eating my – Do you see where I'm going with this?

ELLIOT. I do.

JODI. Ok. And now that *child* is *engaged* to my *husband* – ex-husband, whatever – my Greg. I mean, *my* Greg. I mean, how fucked up is that?

ELLIOT. It's –

JODI. I know, believe me, I know. And everyone I care about, on this planet, stood around last night and pretended that what they have, is real. That the reason Greg and Misty are together isn't because she has big tits. On a tiny little frame. Wonder how that miracle of science occurred. A hundred and ten pounds and tits out to here. She's got that, and he's got a big bank account – full of my money, I might add, money *I* earned, slaving away at the goddamn firm, while he was growing *almonds*, when he was pretending to be a *farmer*, until that failed, like everything he ever touched – Farmer Greg – but, no. We're supposed to pretend that what they have, is love. Greg is genuinely in love with – what do they even talk about? I want to see the transcripts! What does a fifty-year-old father of two with bad knees and intense ear hair – which I trimmed by the way, *I* trimmed that nasty, coarse – what do they talk about? And do you think *Misty* trims his ear hair?

(She pauses, as if waiting for **ELLIOT** *to answer.)*

ELLIOT. Is that a rhetorical question?

JODI. No! It's not! I know she doesn't. I just... I quit. I quit. I just. Fucking. Qui– and I'm not – I mean, I get it. I'm not a *moron*. Twenty-four-year-old pussy tastes fresher than the pussy of someone in her very early... early forties...

(Quick beat.)

Mid-forties...

(Quick beat.)

Whatever. The tits are perkier, the ass is more grab-able, her like natural state of being is wet. I get it. Guess what? Twenty-year-old dick tastes better than fifty-year-old dick. Ok? It just does. But like, some of us recognize, I mean, I recognize, I mean, can't we all recognize there is more to life than that? There has GOT to be more to life than sex with a hot young thing – which, I am willing to admit Misty is, I'm a bigger person, I am willing to admit – but as good as that is, it can't top *everything* else. Can it? I mean, it can't.

Can it?

I just... Fuck.

You look great, though.

(Beat.)

ELLIOT. Honey, I – I've been there. Divorce is brutal. Divorce is –

JODI. Oh my god I can't listen to you of all people tell me divorce is brutal.

ELLIOT. But I've been through it, your mother and I –

JODI. Uh uh uh, no, I did not come home to re-litigate your divorce, no no no no no. No. Just – just pat me on the back and say, "There there," that's all you have to do.

(*ELLIOT is not a touchy-feely person, but he pats JODI's back.*)

ELLIOT. There. There.

JODI. Thank you. I really appreciate the support. It is so comforting.

(*JEFF, a houseboy, enters with a tray: a glass pitcher of water with slices of orange and lemon, some fruit, a croissant. He sets it out on the table. JODI watches him. He's attractive.*)

Thank you... so much.

JEFF. My pleasure.

(*He exits as ORSOLYA, a housekeeper, enters and carries Jodi's wheeled suitcase upstairs.*)

JODI. Is he new?

ELLIOT. No, that's Jeff.

JODI. Oh, right. He's nice.

(*She reaches for a croissant. ELLIOT puts it back and hands her a piece of fruit.*)

I am *without* joy right now. Back off.

(*ELLIOT backs off.*)

I really don't need you calling me fat.

ELLIOT. Did I say one word?

JODI. You were implying. You think I put on weight?

(*ELLIOT's about to respond.*)

Say no.

ELLIOT. No.

JODI. All you have to say is, "Jodi honey, you look terrific."

ELLIOT. But you just came off a flight?

(Quick beat.)

JODI. "Jodi honey, you look terrific."

ELLIOT.	**JODI.**
Jodi honey, you look terrific.	Forget it. FORGET it. Just drop it.

*(**JODI** picks the croissant back up and starts to pull it apart.)*

JODI. It's actually very healthy to comfort eat a little. My therapist told me that, so...

ELLIOT. You can just as easily comfort eat an apple.

JODI. Yeah but you can't pull an apple apart like this, you know? Which is so fun. And makes you feel like you're really accomplishing something.

(Beat.)

ELLIOT. Listen honey. I am... glad you're here, really I am, but I want to make sure you're very clear on the fact that there are to be no other surprises this weekend.

JODI. What do you mean?

ELLIOT. No surprise party. No, no cowboys jumping out of cakes –

JODI. No, there are no cowboys jumping out of cakes.

ELLIOT. Because you understand, that would be my worst nightmare.

JODI. Yes, I know. You don't have to worry. I'm way too consumed with myself right now to go to that kind of trouble for anyone.

ELLIOT. Excellent.

JODI. If you wanna have a birthday dinner, just the family, then fine, and if not, then we –

ELLIOT. No dinner.

JODI. Fine.

(Quick beat.)

ELLIOT. What do you mean, the "family"?

JODI. The family. Us. Our family.

(Beat.)

ELLIOT. Jodi?

JODI. Daddy?

ELLIOT. You're up to something.

JODI. I'm not up to anything.

ELLIOT. Then what is that look?

JODI. What look?

ELLIOT. You've got that look.

JODI. What look?

ELLIOT. That look.

JODI. I don't have any look, there's no look, I don't know what you're talking about with the look, there's no look.

(Quick beat.)

There's no look!

(Beat.)

Benji's coming.

ELLIOT. Christ, Jodi.

JODI. Happy Birthday!

ELLIOT. You never listen.

JODI. I listen, but I wasn't gonna let you turn seventy by yourself.

ELLIOT. But I said I didn't want to do anything.

JODI. Well people don't always say what they mean.

ELLIOT. Well I do!

JODI. Well boo fucking hoo. You'll have to turn seventy surrounded by people who love you. How awful.

ELLIOT. That better be it.

JODI. That's it, but I really don't understand why you're so opposed to having a little –

ELLIOT. Because I am.

JODI. But it's nice to let people celebrate your, you know, your milestone.

ELLIOT. It's not an achievement, to not die.

JODI. Fine.

ELLIOT. And no more surprises.

JODI. Fine.

ELLIOT. Promise?

JODI. I promise.

ELLIOT. Grayson's not coming?

JODI. My nightmare child? My punishment? My crucible? No. I wanted him to, but his grades are... beyond abysmal. Thacher has him on, what do you call it, academic probation? Ugh. But my Benji's coming. He had to fly back through New York anyway. Why he had to do his study abroad in Budapest, I'll never know. Happy healthy children go to London, or Paris, or *Australia*. My son goes to Hungary, to find his roots. But I'm not gonna worry about that, he's coming tonight, that's what matters. So just, relax. Stop acting so crazy.

ELLIOT. *I'm* acting crazy?

JODI. Do not – I cannot handle insinuations that I'm acting crazy right now. I am – I am holding on by a very thin thread, Daddy. A very thin thread. I'm holding on by a thread this thin:

(*She holds up an imagined thread.*)

Can you see that? No you can't and you wanna know why? Because that is a fucking thin fucking thread. Everything is blowing up at work, I'm not sleeping, my kids are both off at school, my ex-husband is getting remarried to a spinner, Trixie's gonna die any day now, I'm all alone in –

ELLIOT. Who's Trixie?

JODI. My cat.

ELLIOT. Oh, right.

JODI. Thank god you're having a birthday because right now, I need a reason – any reason, whatsoever, to celebrate *something*. So just fucking go along with it, ok?

*(**ORSOLYA** returns from upstairs as **JEFF** enters and touches his watch, reminding **ELLIOT** he has an appointment.)*

Oh Orsolya, could you get the bedroom ready on the fourth floor? Benji's coming tonight, he loves it up there.

ORSOLYA. Of course.

(She goes back upstairs.)

JODI. Thank you.

ELLIOT. I have a 10:30, I have to call into. It won't take long.

JODI. This is what retirement looks like?

ELLIOT. I'm still the chairman.

JODI. Emeritus.

ELLIOT. That's right.

JODI. So they don't *(Unspoken: need you.)* – Isn't that just, like, a title?

ELLIOT. No it's not just, like, a title, Jodi.

JODI. Oh.

ELLIOT. I am the one – I am still the one who puts out the fires.

JODI. And what fires are, like, blazing today?

ELLIOT. The men's shirts.

JODI. Oh?

ELLIOT. They're too white.

JODI. What color are they supposed to be?

ELLIOT. White. But the ones they're proposing are, too white.

*(He exits with **JEFF**. **JODI** opens her purse, takes out a compact, checks herself where mascara may have run.)*

*(**TREY** enters. **JODI** notices him the way rich people notice the help, which is to say, she knows he's there but does nothing to acknowledge him.)*

TREY. El?

JODI. He's on a call.

TREY. Oh.

Who're you?

JODI. Jodi.

TREY. Jodi?

JODI. Elliot's daughter.

TREY. Oh right, yeah I forgot he had a kid.

JODI. I'm the kid.

> (**TREY** *goes over to the coffee table, inspects the breakfast, picks up an apple, and takes a bite.*)

Do you work here?

TREY. Excuse me?

JODI. Do you work here?

TREY. No, I'm Trey.

JODI. Ok. Do you work here?

TREY. No, I live here.

JODI. I thought Daddy didn't do live-in anymore?

TREY. No, I live here.

We're partners.

JODI. Who's partners?

TREY. Me and Elliot.

JODI. Partners? Like, business partners?

TREY. No, partners. Like, partner partners.

> (**JODI** *starts laughing.*)

JODI. Sorry. Oh god.

TREY. Why're you laughing?

JODI. Partners? That's very sweet.

TREY. I live here. I'm Trey.

JODI. Well, ok, Trey, nice to meet you, honey.

TREY. Me and El are partners.

JODI. El? Ok. Well. Do me a favor? My son is coming later tonight, he's probably the same age as you, actually, but we're gonna be having some much-needed family time, so it'd be good if you stayed at your place this weekend, ok?

TREY. I don't have a place. This is my place.

JODI. Then, go stay with friends. But this is a family weekend.

TREY. But I live here.

JODI. Thank you, Trey.

(She puts away her compact.)

TREY. I'm his partner.

JODI. Yeah, Daddy's had a LOT of partners. Though he's never called them partners before, that is definitely a first.

TREY. He didn't tell me you were coming.

JODI. He didn't know.

You know it's Daddy's birthday tomorrow?

TREY. It is?

JODI. Yeah.

TREY. Oh yeah he mentioned it, like maybe like, a couple weeks ago, but he was like, he didn't wanna –

JODI. To do anything for it. Right.

His *seventieth* birthday.

TREY. Oh.

JODI. Yeah.

TREY. That's a big one.

JODI. Yes it is.

Look, I don't mean to burst your bubble, cause you seem like a nice enough kid, but Daddy cycles through boys pretty fast, so... for your own dignity, I wouldn't go around telling people you're partners.

How old are you even?

TREY. Twenty.

JODI. That's the same age as my son.

TREY. Ok?

JODI. Elliot's *grandson*.

TREY. El's a grandpa?

JODI. Yes he is. I would have thought you'd have known that, seeing as you're partners and all.

TREY. No I knew, it's just funny to think of Elliot *Isaac* as a grandpa.

JODI. Yes it is, isn't it.

(**ELLIOT** *returns.*)

Daddy! You didn't tell me you had a partner?

ELLIOT. So you two met. Good.

JODI. Yes, I met your *partner*.

ELLIOT. Good.

JODI. I don't know what to say. Mazel Tov?

TREY. Ready, Grandpa?

ELLIOT. Excuse me?

TREY. Nothing babes.

ELLIOT. Let's go.

JODI. Where you going, partner?

TREY. Motorcycle lessons.

JODI. Motorcycle lessons?

TREY. On the West Side Highway. It's fun as hell.

JODI. Daddy? *You're* taking motorcycle lessons?

ELLIOT. Occasionally. It's... fun as hell!

JODI. Don't you think that's a little dangerous?

TREY. It's not dangerous at all, it's –

JODI. Daddy shouldn't be on motorcycles. Not at his age –

TREY. They make you wear a helmet.

JODI. Well, I don't think Daddy's gonna have his lesson today.

ELLIOT. Why wouldn't I have my lesson?

JODI. Because? I just flew across the country to be with you?

ELLIOT. Ok...

JODI. So maybe we could send the party boys home and spend some time toget–

TREY. I live here. You don't have to be so Byzantine.

(**JODI** *is a little stunned to hear* **TREY** *use such a big word.*)

ELLIOT. Trey lives here.

JODI. It's the first I'm hearing of it.

ELLIOT. No it's not.

JODI. Yeah, it kind of is, yeah. It is.

ELLIOT. No, I told you about Trey. You're wrong.

JODI. Well, I guess I didn't clock it then. It's hard to keep track of all your boys.

TREY. You didn't tell me tomorrow was your birthday.

ELLIOT. Of course I did.

TREY. No I know, but you didn't tell me you were turning seventy.

JODI. Did he forget to mention that? Yes. Daddy was born October 4th, 1944, just as World War II was really getting crazy!

ELLIOT. Jodi?

TREY. We should do something for your birthday though –

JODI. I agree, Trey. I completely agree. But Daddy is being totally Byzantine!

ELLIOT. Trey? Wait for me outside.

TREY. But we should have a party. You never want to party.

ELLIOT. Trey?

(*Beat.*)

TREY. Nice to meet you.

(**JODI** *fake smiles at* **TREY.**)

Please, make yourself at home.

(*He exits.*)

JODI. Make yourself at home? Nice.

ELLIOT. What do you want from me?

JODI. I don't know, maybe to not have you run off to a, a what, a motorcycle lesson the second I show up.

ELLIOT. You can't expect the world to drop everything because you decided to breeze in –

JODI. I am not expecting the world to drop everyth– and I am not *breezing* in – all I want – I would think a retired, single man who doesn't see his daughter that often could –

ELLIOT. I am not single.

JODI. You're – I can't, I – I honestly can't with you and your latest plaything.

ELLIOT. Don't be an unterhitzer.

JODI. I'm not even! I said Mazel Tov. That's supportive.

ELLIOT. How about you stop referring to Trey as my plaything, ok?

JODI. Then how about you stop referring to him as your *partner*. Ok?

ELLIOT. You want to come visit, you need to get out of LA? Fine. You're always welcome. But I have a life here, you do not get to come and trash that life.

JODI. Oh slow your roll Daddy, no one's trashing anything. Live your life, I don't care, I never have. All I want is *one* weekend where there aren't little interlopers running around. I just need one weekend with like, people who actually mean something to each other, who *love* each other. That's all I'm asking.

(**ELLIOT** *begins to exit.*)

ELLIOT. Antony's in his office, if you need anything.

JODI. Oh gee thanks. Ok, well. I'll try and make myself at home. In my home.

ELLIOT. We'll go for dinner tonight, when Benji gets here. Ok? Ok.

(*He walks away.*)

JODI. Really, Daddy?

ELLIOT. Really what?

(**JODI** *says nothing.* **ELLIOT** *exits.*)

(**ORSOLYA** *enters to clear breakfast.*)

JODI. What's uhm... what do you make of them?

(Quick beat.)

ORSOLYA. They're in love.

> *(**JODI** lets out a short, sharp, guttural sound; a suppressed laugh.)*

JODI. Yeah that's... that's not the word for what that is.

> *(She thinks, then drags herself upstairs.)*

Scene Two

(Later. Evening.)

*(**TREY** is dressed up, maybe tight dress pants, great shoes, white button-down shirt rolled up at the sleeves. He sits on the couch, texting, scratching his balls.)*

*(Then **ELLIOT** enters, also well dressed.)*

TREY. Hey babes.

ELLIOT. She's driving me crazy.

TREY. So kick her to the curb.

ELLIOT. That's not how family works.

TREY. 'S how my family does. My mama never had a problem kicking me out.

ELLIOT. Well. I'm not your mama.

TREY. No you're not. Yo, we going soon? I'm hungry as fuck.

ELLIOT. As soon as Ben gets here.

TREY. Oh. Right. Grandpa.

ELLIOT. Stop.

TREY. Sorry babes. No I'm pumped to meet your grandson. Is he cool?

ELLIOT. No, Trey. He's not cool.

TREY. Oh. But is he like, fun?

ELLIOT. No. He's not fun. He's spoiled. Very spoiled.

TREY. Oh, snap. Hey, what time'll dinner be over?

ELLIOT. We're not going out tonight.

TREY. I didn't say I was.

ELLIOT. We're coming home when dinner's over.

TREY. You can come home.

ELLIOT. No Trey. *We* are coming home.

TREY. But it's Saturday, I'm not fucking sitting around on a Saturday night. That's like –

ELLIOT. *We* are coming home.

TREY. But Bobby said there's gonna be people out –

ELLIOT. Who's Bobby?

TREY. You know Bobby. My friend, Bobby. You met Bobby.

ELLIOT. I never met Bobby.

TREY. Yes you did. You met Bobby. He's got that tattoo of the snake that goes from…

> *(He puts his hand under his own collar and draws a snake up his neck to behind his ear.)*

ELLIOT. Oh. Right.

TREY. Yeah and he's going to the Boom Boom Room, everyone's gonna be there, and like –

ELLIOT. Do not test me tonight. Ok? My family is here, just be good.

TREY. I'm bein' good but you're like making up all these rules, it's fucking arbitrary as fuck –

ELLIOT. You didn't cuff those correctly.

TREY. What?

> *(**ELLIOT** approaches **TREY** and re-cuffs his sleeves in a precise and exacting manner. **TREY** allows it. **JEFF** passes through.)*

Get me a Diet Coke.

*(To **ELLIOT**.)* You want anything?

> *(**ELLIOT** shakes his head no. **JEFF** exits.)*

ELLIOT. I want you to be my good boy tonight, ok?

TREY. I'm always good.

ELLIOT. No. You're not.

TREY. Yes I am! Unless I'm being bad, but being bad is like being good, just, in a different way.

JODI. *(Offstage.)* He's here. Three minutes away. Just texted.

> *(We hear **JODI** upstairs.)*

TREY. She's mad uptight yo. What crawled up her ass and died?

ELLIOT. Her husband left her.

TREY. Ok…

ELLIOT. For another woman.

TREY. Oh.

ELLIOT. A significantly younger woman.

TREY. Oh shit.

ELLIOT. She caught them in bed. In her bedroom.

TREY. Oh shiiiiiiit.

ELLIOT. It's not funny, Trey.

TREY. I ain't laughing about that, it's something else I'm just...

Sorry.

(JEFF has returned with the Coke, waiting.)

Can you just set it down?

(JEFF puts the Coke down on the table.)

Use a fucking coaster.

ELLIOT. Trey.

TREY. He never uses a fucking coaster, it's fucking ridiculous.

ELLIOT. Thank you, Jeff.

JEFF. My pleasure.

(He puts the Coke on a coaster, then exits.)

TREY. *(Breathily whispered.)* My pleasure.

ELLIOT. You have to be nice to the people who work here.

TREY. I am. I'm super nice. To the ones who deserve it.

ELLIOT. He's never done anything to you.

TREY. I don't like him in the house, I tole you that –

ELLIOT. He's a good worker.

TREY. No he ain't, he's a fucktard. He's fucking stupid as fuck.

ELLIOT. That's enough Trey.

TREY. And he's fuckin' fugly. I hate his face, I hate lookin' at it.

ELLIOT. That's enough.

TREY. I get it, he needs a job, but why *you* gotta give him one? There's still Pizza Hut? Let him deliver frickin pizzas at frickin Pizza Hut why he gotta work here?

ELLIOT. That is enough, Trey.

TREY. I cain't believe you ever stuck your dick in that nasty washed up, used up nasty...

ELLIOT. Trey.

TREY. It's a miracle your dick didn't fall off.

ELLIOT. *Who* are you texting?

TREY. No one!!

ELLIOT. Is that Bobby?

TREY. No it ain't Bobby it ain't nobody, it's none of your damn business so –

> (**ELLIOT** *grabs* **TREY***'s phone. Once the phone is in* **ELLIOT***'s hand, it's his. Though* **TREY** *may want it back, he makes no effort to take it.)*

Gimme my phone what the – gimme my –

ELLIOT. Don't tell me you're not texting Bobby when you're texting Bobby.

TREY. Can you just chill out? He's my friend, that's it. Don't take my phone like that.

ELLIOT. Don't test me, Trey.

TREY. Or what, huh? What?

> (*In one breathless motion,* **TREY** *pulls his shirt from his back, over his head, and throws it somewhere. Then he sits.* **ELLIOT** *goes to the shirt, picks it up gently, folds it, and places it next to* **TREY** *before sitting near him. After a beat,* **TREY***, shirtless, nestles himself into* **ELLIOT***.)*

I don't want to fight.

> (*After a beat,* **ELLIOT** *gently runs the back of his fingers against* **TREY***'s bicep and forearm, gazing at it, studying it, as if the answer to some ancient question lies buried under the blue veins of* **TREY***'s arm.)*

You like that.

ELLIOT. I'd like to have sheets made from your skin.

TREY. I bet you would.

ELLIOT. I'd like to sleep in a bed with sheets made from your skin.

TREY. *(Sing-song.)*
CREEPY.

> *(**ELLIOT** smiles.)*

ELLIOT. If I made a line of sheets, from your skin? I'd make millions.

TREY. That'd be cool, ta have my own line of sheets...

ELLIOT. Millions.

TREY. You have millions.

ELLIOT. Maybe I want more.

TREY. You always want more.

> *(**JEFF** enters. The men make no effort to break apart.)*

JEFF. I believe your grandson just arrived.

ELLIOT. Oh good, thank you.

TREY. Thank you for my Coke.

JEFF. My pleasure.

> *(He exits.)*

ELLIOT. That was very nice of you, Trey.

TREY. I know.

Toldja I was good.

> *(Beat. **TREY** rises and begins to put his shirt back on.)*

It's so weird, cause like, I never do nothing for my ass, you know, in the gym or whatever, but it's just like just naturally just like juicy, I got a juicy ass. Everyone's always like, how did you get that ass like that, but I never have a answer, cause it's just naturally this way.

BENJAMIN. *(Offstage.)* Hello?

ELLIOT. *(To **TREY**.)* You be good now.

TREY. You be fucking good.

(**BENJAMIN** *enters. He's twenty. He's tired. He's got an enormous suitcase, which* **ORSOLYA** *wheels behind her.*)

ELLIOT. Benji. You made it.

BENJAMIN. *(Already annoyed.)* Hi, Elliot.

ELLIOT. How was your trip?

BENJAMIN. Mom put me on coach.

ELLIOT. Ben, this is Trey. Trey, Ben.

TREY. Sup?

(**BENJAMIN** *looks at* **TREY** *but doesn't respond.*)

ELLIOT. Will you take that to the south bedroom, on the fourth floor?

(**ORSOLYA** *nods, then takes the suitcase, which is way too heavy for her, upstairs.*)

BENJAMIN. Do I have to be on the fourth floor? I hate it up there.

ELLIOT. Your mom said you like it there.

BENJAMIN. She just said that cause she hates it up there. It gets so hot.

ELLIOT. Then, open a window.

BENJAMIN. That doesn't do anything.

ELLIOT. Jodi! Your son is here!

JODI. *(From upstairs.)* Hi hi hi I'll be down in two seconds, I'm just dealing with this client.

(**BENJAMIN** *is staring at* **TREY**.)

TREY. What?

BENJAMIN. What? Nothing, sorry, just, you look familiar.

TREY. I get that a lot.

ELLIOT. How's school? Benjamin is studying abroad in Budapest this semester.

TREY. What's that?

BENJAMIN. What's what?

TREY. Studying abroad?

BENJAMIN. Didn't they have study abroad at your college?

TREY. I didn't go to college not all of us went to college. Shit.

ELLIOT. The last time I was in Budapest, we opened the store on the, the main shopping street there, and –

BENJAMIN. Váci Street?

ELLIOT. That's the one. I flew over for the opening, got in the car to go to the ceremony, and, we couldn't move. There were people, everywhere. I thought maybe someone was assassinated, some protest, a government shutdown, something. Cause people were lining the streets, far as the eye could see. But then the driver said, "Didn't you hear? Elliot Isaac is opening his store today." When I tell you the crowd stretched more than two miles in both directions. I'm not making that up. Usually, you open a store, there's a few people, some cultural what-have-yous, attachés, but nothing like this. I said, "Is this what it's always like here?" No. They never had a crowd like that before. They told me. This was after the wall came down, everyone wanted American clothing. I said, but you have lots of stores here that sell American clothing. They said, but your clothing *is* America. We sold out in five hours, the entire inventory. Everything.

BENJAMIN. *(The opposite of impressed.)* Oh wow.

ELLIOT. Afterwards, I get back in the car, and at that point he realized who he had been driving, he said, why didn't you tell me? I said, because. That's not who I am.

> *(Quick beat. **ELLIOT** waits for **BENJAMIN** to say something, but he is silent.)*

I think the store is still there.

BENJAMIN. It is. I've walked by.

ELLIOT. How's it look?

BENJAMIN. Like a store.

ELLIOT. Ok.

TREY. Orsolya's from Hungary.

BENJAMIN. Who?

TREY. Orsolya? She's worked here for like – she just took your bag upstairs?

BENJAMIN. Oh.

TREY. She's from Hungary too. She's been teaching me. Maybe we can practice later.

BENJAMIN. Oh, I'm not learning Hungarian. I'm studying queer theory, mostly... so.

ELLIOT. That's...

BENJAMIN. It's gay shit, Elliot. It's *super* gay.

ELLIOT. Uh huh.

TREY. Yeah I been studying Hungarian, I wanted to check it out when we was abroad but we ran out of time.

BENJAMIN. You came to Hungary?

ELLIOT. No. Italy.

TREY. Yeah, like last month maybe. Venizia, Florence, Roma. Milan.

BENJAMIN. I didn't know you were in Europe.

ELLIOT. I go to Europe all the time.

TREY. It was pretty cool. I rode in a gondola, I almost fell in but then I didn't.

BENJAMIN. You could have visited me.

ELLIOT. You're studying. There was no need to bother you.

BENJAMIN. My classes are easy. I could have met you in Italy.

ELLIOT. I didn't know.

BENJAMIN. You would have known if you'd asked me.

ELLIOT. Ok. Next time.

BENJAMIN. Well. I'm only there for like two more months, so...

ELLIOT. I didn't know you were going abroad until your mother told me.

BENJAMIN. I told you –

ELLIOT. No. Your mother told me.

BENJAMIN. That's not true. Elliot, I called you, I –

ELLIOT. You didn't. It doesn't matter now.

BENJAMIN. Yes I did, I –

TREY. You call him Elliot?

BENJAMIN. What? Yeah. I –

TREY. But ain't he your grandpa? Why don't you call him Gramps or something?

BENJAMIN. Because I don't.

ELLIOT. Jodi! Let's go!

(**ORSOLYA** *is walking back downstairs.*)

TREY. Hodge vodge, babe! That's Hungarian for wassup.

ORSOLYA. Hello Trey.

TREY. We gotta teach this dude Hungarian, he lives there but he don't even speak it.

ORSOLYA. You live in Hungary?

BENJAMIN. Oh god no. I'm just studying there.

TREY. Yeah but I speak better Hungarian than him cause he's just doing queer theory, that's it.

ORSOLYA. Uh huh. Well I hope you have nice time there, it's a beautiful country.

BENJAMIN. Yeah, it's ok. I mean, I'm glad our family left when they did, right? Or I would not be here now.

TREY. Where would you be?

BENJAMIN. Uhm, dead. I mean, the Hungarians were like, pretty enthusiastic collaborators with Nazis, and like, even today they're still deeply, deeply *(Unspoken: antisemitic.)* ... but I'm sure your family is like, lovely.

TREY. Yeah that's my girl. We're both country boys, except she's not a boy. But she grew up in the country too, but she didn't even have running water where she lived and I did so that's like one big difference between us –

ELLIOT. Let Orsolya get back to work, Trey.

BENJAMIN. I'm sorry, uhm, did you bring my bag upstairs?

ORSOLYA. Yes, I put in south bedroom. Fourth floor.

BENJAMIN. I actually need – it's mostly laundry, dirty laundry, I –

ELLIOT. You brought your dirty clothes to Horatio Street, from Hungary?

BENJAMIN. Laundry in Budapest is an actual nightmare. But, I can do it, I just didn't get a –

ORSOLYA. We can do for you.

BENJAMIN. Oh, really?

ORSOLYA. Is no problem.

BENJAMIN. Thanks.

ORSOLYA. Is no problem.

> *(She walks back upstairs.)*

BENJAMIN. We're studying him, actually.

ELLIOT. Who?

BENJAMIN. Horatio Alger. Isn't Horatio Street named for him?

ELLIOT. I don't know. I don't think so. I don't know.

TREY. Who's that?

ELLIOT. Horatio Alger? The rags to riches guy.

TREY. Rags to riches?

ELLIOT. He went from rags... to riches.

BENJAMIN. Which is like, I mean, everyone's called Elliot the Horatio Alger of Brooklyn for so long, but most people don't even know who he was anymore. He's actually a really fascinating guy, Alger. Did you know he was a pedophile?

ELLIOT. Uh, no, I did not. Trey? Enough texting.

TREY. Oh my god! I'm not even.

ELLIOT. That's a good – good.

> *(**JODI** enters. She goes right to **BENJAMIN**, hugs him and doesn't let go.)*

JODI. Hi my sweetie-sweetie. I was just dealing with – that client needs to get a fucking life already – I'm so glad you're here, sweetie.

BENJAMIN. Mom, I just saw you in LA, yesterday.

JODI. But only for like five minutes.

BENJAMIN. We spent like three hours together.

(**JODI** *kisses his cheek.* **TREY** *exits into the kitchen.*)

BENJAMIN. Mom. It's ok. Relax.

ELLIOT. Don't eat now, Trey.

TREY. *(Offstage.)* I'm not!

JODI. You look so good, Benji! Doesn't he look good? They're feeding you over there.

BENJAMIN. Please don't call me fat.

JODI. What? I would never. I'm just glad you found things to eat. They have enough gluten-free options for you?

BENJAMIN. I haven't starved to death yet, no.

JODI. You haven't starved to death! You're so funny. He's so funny. Oh my god I'm so happy you're here. The normal people are here now.

(**TREY** *returns, licking his fingers.*)

Did Benji tell you he's learning Yiddish?

ELLIOT. No. He just said he's doing the queer.

BENJAMIN. Queer theory. And I'm not learning Yiddish, it's Yiddish culture.

ELLIOT. That's an odd combination.

BENJAMIN. It's actually not. There's actually like nine other Yiddish homos in my program, so –

JODI. Don't use that word.

BENJAMIN. What, homo?

JODI. Please. I hate it.

BENJAMIN. You hate it?

JODI. It's derogatory.

BENJAMIN. No it's not.

TREY. What's Yiddish?

ELLIOT. It's an old language no one speaks anymore.

BENJAMIN. Grandma Sylvia speaks Yiddish.

ELLIOT. Grandma Sylvia doesn't speak anymore. Period.

JODI. Not at all?

ELLIOT. Not really.

TREY. Who's Grandma Sylvia?

JODI.   **ELLIOT.**

His mother, partner.   My mother.

TREY. You have a mama still? Damn, she must be old as hell!

JODI. Excuse me?

TREY. What?

JODI. She should come to your birthday dinner tomorrow.

ELLIOT. There is no dinner tomorrow.

JODI. Yes Daddy, we discussed this. A family dinner, remember? For your birthday. Just the family.

ELLIOT. Whatever, but you're not to bring Mom.

JODI. Why not?

ELLIOT. Because. She can't speak. She can't eat. She takes her meals through a straw. She's not up for anything like that.

JODI. Well, we'll go see her tomorrow. Maybe she'll be feeling up for it. Maybe if Benji talks to her in Yiddish, she might –

ELLIOT. She won't.

JODI. How do you know?

ELLIOT. Because I know.

BENJAMIN. For the nine hundredth time, I'm not learning Yiddish.

JODI. But you're learning words, right? Yiddish has the best words. Schlep! And...

    (Can't remember any.)

So many great words. Oh, this makes me so happy. It's like old times. All of us together, talking in Yiddish.

TREY. Babes? I'm like so starving, it's almost eight thirty.

ELLIOT. Let's go.

JODI. Wow. Trey. That is some watch.

TREY. Thanks.

JODI. What is it?

TREY. The GMT Master II.

JODI. That's a Rolex?

TREY. Yeah.

JODI. Wow. And is that –

TREY. White gold. Eighteen karats.

JODI. Uh huh. And are those –

TREY. Diamonds. Yeah. Real ones.

JODI. Wow. That is absolutely stunning.

TREY. Thanks.

JODI. That must've cost a pretty penny.

TREY. Four fifty.

JODI. Four hundred and fifty thousand dollars?

TREY. Yeah.

JODI. Woooow.

TREY. It was a present.

BENJAMIN. Nice present.

JODI. I'll say.

TREY. Yeah. Thanks babes.

JODI. What was it a present for?

TREY. Just cuz.

JODI. Just cuz?

TREY. Yeah. Just cuz El loves me.

JODI. Just cuz El loves you. Wow.

TREY. Yeah. He's like a romantic but, I am too so, it works.

JODI. Huh. That's a side of you I've never seen.

TREY. That's cause you're his daughter. It's different if it's partners. Right babes?

ELLIOT. That's right. Ok let's go eat. You hungry, Benji?

> *(The following dialogue is rapid-fire, as only a family can communicate with each other.)*

JODI. Daddy?

BENJAMIN. I guess.

JODI. I'm speechless.

ELLIOT. We're going to Per Se, you *guess*?

JODI. Did you check if they have gluten-free options for Benji?

ELLIOT. I'm sure they do.

JODI. But did you check?

BENJAMIN. I'll be fine.

ELLIOT. The car's out front. Let's go.

BENJAMIN. How do you know?

TREY. Gluten free is such a hoax.

JODI. Excuse me –

ELLIOT. Antony texted me before.

JODI. Benjamin's gluten issues are not a *hoax*.

BENJAMIN. He texts you now?

ELLIOT. It's easier.

JODI. Daddy!

TREY. El likes the help to be invisible.

BENJAMIN. I… know –

JODI. I wouldn't wish Benji's gluten issues on my worst enemy, not my worst enemy.

BENJAMIN. Mom. I'll be fine.

ELLIOT. Come on, let's go.

JODI. But what if they don't have something for you to eat?

BENJAMIN. I. Will. Be. Fine.

> *(He exits.)*

JODI. After you.

TREY. Ladies first.

> *(**JODI** decides she can't talk to her dad now, and exits.)*

You don't have to tell me. I know.

ELLIOT. What do you know?

TREY. Be good.

ELLIOT. And are you going to be?

TREY. I'll be a perfect gentleman.

Scene Three

(Deep into that same night. Around two in the morning.)

*(**BENJAMIN** sits upright on the couch, looking at his phone. The TV is on, on the wall in front of him, which we can't see, but there's no volume. We're with him for a moment. Then, footsteps. **JODI** enters, **BENJAMIN** fumbles with his phone.)*

JODI. Can't sleep?

BENJAMIN. Not really.

JODI. Me neither. Maybe you're jet-lagged too?

BENJAMIN. Yeah maybe.

JODI. What you watching?

BENJAMIN. Oh, I don't know, nothing.

JODI. There's no volume.

BENJAMIN. I'm not watching, I just... wanted something to be on.

JODI. Ugh, this show is for morons. Are you playing on your phone?

BENJAMIN. What?

JODI. I just saw you on your phone. Are you on Grindr?

BENJAMIN. *Mom.*

JODI. I know what Grindr is honey, I'm alive in the world. Are you –

BENJAMIN. Mom I really don't want to do this with you.

JODI. That's for hook-ups, right? To find boys who –

BENJAMIN. Mom, please.

JODI. Any cuties?

BENJAMIN. Mom can you not?

JODI. What? I'm just –

BENJAMIN. I hate when you do your "cool mom" routine.

JODI. I'm not doing a cool mom routine, I'm just –

BENJAMIN. Just stop, please, ok?

JODI. I hope this goes without saying, but you know you
have to be safe, you know that –

BENJAMIN. Oh my god, Mom.

JODI. It's great to meet new people, but they'll lie to you to
get you in bed. You're a gorgeous young man –

BENJAMIN. I'm not gorgeous –

JODI. You're gorgeous, and they'll say all sorts of things,
and if you want to go to bed with them, that's fine, just
please, please be safe.

BENJAMIN. MOM. Swear to God.

JODI. You don't believe in God.

BENJAMIN. I'll start. Don't test me. Let's just drop this,
RIGHT now.

(Quick beat.)

JODI. I think I'm a little gassy from dinner.

BENJAMIN. Mom.

JODI. Sorry.

BENJAMIN. Gross.

(Quick beat.)

JODI. You're cute.

BENJAMIN. Thank you.

JODI. I really miss you.

BENJAMIN. We literally just had dinner together.

JODI. You know what I mean. I'm really glad you're here.

BENJAMIN. Ok.

JODI. Are you glad you came?

BENJAMIN. No.

JODI. But you had to fly to LA for Dad's engagement party
anyway, right?

BENJAMIN. Right.

JODI. Are you glad you flew in for that?

BENJAMIN. He made me.

JODI. But you're glad you did?

BENJAMIN. Yeah, I'm really glad I did.

JODI. Good. Good. I'm glad.

And how was the party? You didn't even tell me. Did you wind up having fun?

BENJAMIN. It was fine.

JODI. It was fine, but was it fun?

BENJAMIN. It was fun.

JODI. A lot of fun, or...

BENJAMIN. Yeah. A lot of fun. Yeah.

JODI. Good. Good.

    (Beat.)

Who came, exactly?

BENJAMIN. Mom! I don't know.

JODI. Right, but like, who exactly?

BENJAMIN. Mom.

JODI. I'm just curious who came.

BENJAMIN. Dad's family.

JODI. Who specifically?

BENJAMIN. All of them.

JODI. Frank flew in for it?

BENJAMIN. Yeah, Uncle Frank was there.

JODI. What about Phil?

BENJAMIN. He was there, too.

JODI. Did he bring what's-her-name?

BENJAMIN. No. They broke up.

JODI. Really? Why?

BENJAMIN. I don't know, I didn't ask.

JODI. I knew that wouldn't last. What about the Rosens, did –

BENJAMIN. Mom. A lot of people were there. Ok?

JODI. Humiliating.

BENJAMIN. Why is that humiliating?

JODI. It's not even the wedding! And your dad is almost fifty, he's done this before. Who has an enormous engagement party for a second marriage?

BENJAMIN. I don't know, I mean, Madison's never been married, it's all new for her, so –

JODI. Oh my god.

BENJAMIN. What?

JODI. Sorry. Nothing.

Nothing.

> *(Quick beat.)*

I thought her name was Misty. I forgot it was Madison. That's like... I knew a girl growing up, she had a *horse* named Madison. She lived in a barn. The whole thing gives me the heebees.

BENJAMIN. Grayson's so weird with her.

JODI. Really? How so?

BENJAMIN. I don't know, he's just like obsessed with her breasts, he talks about them all the time –

JODI. What???

BENJAMIN. Not to her. To me. To me. But still it's like, this woman is gonna be our stepmom, maybe like, don't talk about her breasts so much.

JODI. Oh god. Like father, like son.

Like grandfather, like father, like son. Ugh. Grayson. What are we gonna do with him?

BENJAMIN. I don't know.

JODI. I don't know either.

BENJAMIN. There was also, there was one other part that was weird.

JODI. What?

BENJAMIN. Just like, in the toasts, they kept making jokes about how Madison wasn't, how she wasn't just marrying Dad cause of his – which, I didn't even know, but apparently he has...

JODI. Has what?

BENJAMIN. You know. A really big... like...

> (He implies "penis.")

Like, they were like, Madison's not just marrying you because of your huuuuuuge... and then they'd pause and be like, "personality!" Or because of your very looooooong... yacht! And everyone laughed like the whole room apparently knew, but I never...

> (He looks at JODI. She's remembering Greg's penis, which she hasn't seen in over a year but which brought her more pleasure than maybe anything on this Earth. BENJAMIN gets a sense of this and is silently totally weirded out.)

> (JODI comes back to Earth.)

JODI. Well that is so inappropriate. And what did your father do, when this was happening?

BENJAMIN. He just like, laughed. I mean, what was he supposed to do.

JODI. Ugh. Disgusting.

You're like, the most mature man I know.

BENJAMIN. That's depressing.

JODI. But it's true. I mean, look at the set of examples you've got. Every man you know is dating someone younger, *marrying* someone younger. What message is that sending you and Grayson?

BENJAMIN. I don't know. Date younger.

JODI. Yeah exactly. But that's not the message I want you boys to get.

BENJAMIN. It isn't?

JODI. No. What matters is who somebody is on the inside. That's what matters. Not looks.

BENJAMIN. Oh. Well. I think that message got lost like somewhere around the war over Helen of Troy.

JODI. This world is so fucked.

BENJAMIN. Kind of, yeah.

JODI. But I'm also dazzled that you know about Helen of Troy. I just want to say that.

BENJAMIN. Uhm I think everyone knows about Helen of Troy.

JODI. I doubt that. I doubt *Trey* knows much about Helen of Troy.

BENJAMIN. Yeah, well, I think…

I think Trey did porn.

JODI. There's a fuckin' surprise.

BENJAMIN. No, I mean… I know he's done porn.

JODI. How do you know?

BENJAMIN. Because I've – I know.

JODI. Oh.

BENJAMIN. His name is *Bryce*, on the site.

JODI. *Bryce?*

BENJAMIN. Yeah.

JODI. So you're telling me Daddy's dating a porn star?

BENJAMIN. I wouldn't say star, but… he made a few videos with them. I've… I kind of know that site pretty well, so…

JODI. What's the site? Do I want to know?

BENJAMIN. I don't know, do you?

JODI. Benji! Yes.

BENJAMIN. It's – it's for, where like, straight guys, presumably straight guys, do gay things.

JODI. What do you mean, gay things?

BENJAMIN. Mom. You need me to spell it out?

JODI. So, is Trey straight?

BENJAMIN. I don't know.

JODI. He doesn't seem gay to me.

BENJAMIN. Ok…

(Quick beat.)

JODI. Show me.

(A quick beat. Then **BENJAMIN** *finds the site on his phone and shows it to* **JODI**.*)*

JODI. Oh. My...

BENJAMIN. That's him.

JODI. That's him.

BENJAMIN. And here he's –

JODI. Oh my god is he –

BENJAMIN. Yeah.

JODI. Is that –

BENJAMIN. Yeah.

JODI. Oh my god take that – put that away.

(As she says "put that away" she looks closer at the phone.)

Oh my god. This is HUMILIATING. Humil–

Does *partners* mean something I don't know?

BENJAMIN. I dunno, I guess it's serious.

JODI. A half-a-million-dollar watch? Yeah I'd say that's serious.

BENJAMIN. Elliot's never given me a gift like that.

JODI. Well. Maybe you should start sucking his dick.

BENJAMIN. Mom, that's disgusting.

JODI. Sorry. I just... *what* is Daddy thinking? He's never even had a boyfriend before, as far as I know. It was always a revolving door, they came and went so fast you didn't have time to learn their names. Now he has a *partner*? And it's *Trey*? Who drank like a fish, by the way, an absolute fish. Which can't be good for Daddy's sobriety, but he seemed to find it charming. Although who could tell *what* he's feeling, he's been hitting the botox wayyyyy too hard.

BENJAMIN. You use botox.

JODI. I have *used* botox, I don't use botox. There's a difference.

BENJAMIN. I hate botox.

JODI. Well you can tell me all about it when you're pushing... whatever.

BENJAMIN. Why did you make us come here?

JODI. It's Daddy's birthday.

BENJAMIN. He doesn't give a shit.

JODI. That's not true. It means a lot to him. It's hard for him to show his feelings sometimes, but –

BENJAMIN. Because of all the botox?

He flew to Europe with Trey and didn't even tell me.

JODI. Well, I don't understand that –

BENJAMIN. And when I said I was studying Yiddish culture, he said that was weird. Like –

JODI. Well it is a little strange.

BENJAMIN. A normal grandparent would be like, tell me everything, I love you, I am so proud of you –

JODI. He's proud of you. Believe me, he –

BENJAMIN. I don't give a shit if he's proud of me, that's not the point. The point is, I'm in Budapest, the place our family comes from, and –

JODI. I wouldn't say we're from Budapest. If anything, we come from Brooklyn more than anywhere.

BENJAMIN. Uhm, ok, I'm not even gonna – the point is, what do I get? A story about how when he opened the store they had the biggest crowd in the history of store openings. That's what he like, needs to express. To me. Above all else. What is that?

JODI. I don't know.

BENJAMIN. I'm living in the place our family lived for centuries, and I mean, if you want to see a Jewish name in Hungary, you have to go to a Holocaust memorial. That's where those names are, now. Except for the one exception: Elliot Isaac. Whose name is everywhere. On billboards. On bus stops. And in huge letters, at his flagship store, in the same city his grandparents had to flee because they had a feeling something bad was coming. But there it is, like a huge fuck you to history. And it's not like they've learned anything – the far right is gaining power, antisemitism's on the rise, but that doesn't stop them from buying his jeans and t-shirts and underwear. And I mean, when you think about it, if you wear a pair of his underwear all day, when you take it off, you can see the outline of his name on your body, from where the waistband pressed against you. So the descendents of people who terrorized our family – they get undressed, get ready for bed, and go to sleep with Elliot Isaac's name clinging to their bodies, rising from their skin. A Jew's name. On their actual bodies. It's… a fucking mindfuck. But I didn't get to tell him about that. Because he didn't ask. Because he doesn't give a shit.

JODI. Daddy would have loved to hear about that –

BENJAMIN. He doesn't give a shit. You should have seen how he tensed up when I said *queer* studies tonight. I'm like the living queeny embodiment of all his worst nightmares.

JODI. You are not – Daddy didn't grow up in a time when – Grandma Sylvia would not have asked if there were any cuties online tonight. They used to call him faygele, on the street, when he was a kid. Mommy told me that. Who knows if he would have even married Mommy if he'd been born today. If it weren't for homophobia I might not be alive, and neither would you, so, think about that.

    (Beat.)

I know being here is not – Daddy's not your favorite person. I get it. I know him better than maybe anyone, and even I don't always… he's hard to know, he's been so many things, in one lifetime. Poor, then rich. Religious, then, not. Single, married, divorced, gay, straight… ish. Sober and addicted. He survived the '70s without overdosing, I have no idea how; then he survived the *'80s*, I *really* don't know how. He's been Elliot Isaac the brand, Elliot Isaac the man, Elliot Itzakovich, the scrappy kid from Brooklyn, and *he's* my Dad. He probably shouldn't ever have been a parent, but he is, and... Mommy's gone, Greg is... This is what's left of my family, Benji. And I, uh... I...

(*Beat.*)

BENJAMIN. I think Dad sucks.

JODI. Oh honey.

BENJAMIN. I'm on your side.

JODI. There are no sides – don't take sides – you don't have to take sides.

BENJAMIN. I'm on your side.

JODI. Thanks.

(*Quick beat.*)

I asked Antony to make chicken paillard tomorrow.

BENJAMIN. Ok.

JODI. Benji! Chicken paillard!

BENJAMIN. I don't... should that mean something to me?

JODI. You know about chicken paillard!

BENJAMIN. I don't think so.

JODI. Yes you do. I told you about this.

BENJAMIN. You did?

JODI. Before they split, Mommy and Daddy took a cooking class, on like, the one night in their marriage where they actually did something together, and they learned to make chicken paillard, and then, after they divorced, whenever he came for dinner, Mommy would make it.

BENJAMIN. Oh.

JODI. They didn't get together that often, but sometimes Daddy would come for dinner, and I'd say I had to go to the bathroom, but I'd hide just outside the dining room so I could listen to them talk. We weren't really a family anymore, but it was the closest thing I had, I guess...

I made it for you and Gray once. You both hated it. I probably fucked up the recipe.

BENJAMIN. That's really nice of you, to make dinner for him.

JODI. I'm not cooking it.

BENJAMIN. Still, it's...

> *(Footsteps on the stairs. They look up.* **TREY** *emerges, wearing nothing but his Rolex watch and a jockstrap with the name "Elliot Isaac" emblazoned on the band. He looks at the TV.* **JODI** *and* **BENJAMIN** *are shocked.)*

TREY. Oh I love this show.

> *(He exits into the kitchen. This next conversation is whispered through laughter.)*

JODI. Um, WHAT? Did that just happen?

BENJAMIN. That just happened!

JODI. What the...

BENJAMIN. This is so weird!

JODI. What do we do?

BENJAMIN. I don't know.

JODI. What is he thinking?

BENJAMIN. I don't know!

JODI. I can't believe Daddy makes people wear his own underwear to go to bed.

BENJAMIN. That wasn't underwear. That's a jockstrap.

JODI. What's the difference?

BENJAMIN. I mean, people don't wear jockstraps to go to bed. I don't think.

JODI. Ugh Benji I'm gonna be sick.

> *(***TREY*** returns from the kitchen with a gallon of milk, the fancy kind, in a glass bottle, and a box of cereal. He sits down on the couch near* **JODI** *and* **BENJAMIN** *to watch TV, the box of cereal on his lap, discretely covering him up.)*

Excuse me, we do not sit around naked.

TREY. I'm not.

JODI. Maybe you could put something on?

TREY. I have something on.

JODI. We don't sit around with our bare asses on the couch everyone sits on!

TREY. This is my house, lady, I'll do what I want.

JODI. This is not your house, this is my father's house –

TREY. I live here. It's my house, too.

JODI. You are… this is…

TREY. This show is hilarious.

>   (**JODI** *stands up.*)

JODI. This is *not* what I needed this weekend. Thank you very much, Trey. Benji, I'm sorry about this. Let's go to bed.

>   (*She begins to walk away.* **BENJAMIN** *doesn't move.*)

Benji?

BENJAMIN. I'll be up in a minute.

>   (**JODI***'s eyes bug out. She's horrified, but exits.*)

TREY. Turn it up.

Why's it on so low?

>   (*Beat.*)

What?

BENJAMIN. I didn't say, um…

>   (*He's been holding in his laughter, but now it comes out.*)

TREY. What?

BENJAMIN. Sorry, it's just, this is suuuuper, um…

TREY. God, y'all is so prude, it's like… it's just a naked body. It don't bite. Well…

Gimme your shirt.

BENJAMIN. What?

TREY. This one.

>   (**BENJAMIN** *is wearing an open button-down shirt with a t-shirt visible underneath. He takes off the button-down shirt and hands it to* **TREY**, *who wraps it around his waist.*)

TREY. Better?

BENJAMIN. I mean, it's something.

TREY. Why's it so low?

BENJAMIN. We didn't want to wake anyone.

TREY. Oh, we were awake.

Want some?

(He offers some cereal.)

BENJAMIN. I'm good, thanks.

TREY. Elliot's always like, don't snack at night, but, like, I love to, so...

Turn it up.

BENJAMIN. My mom went to sleep, I don't want to bother her.

TREY. Oh, yeah. She, like, does not like me.

BENJAMIN. Oh. I don't know.

TREY. What'd she say about me?

(Quick beat.)

BENJAMIN. Nothing. Really...

TREY. Nah I can tell. I can read people, if they don't like me, I can always tell. She kept talking over me at dinner like I wasn't there, not looking at me, finally I was just like, fuck it, I'll just sit here and drink my wine. She's mean.

BENJAMIN. She's going through a rough time right now.

TREY. Cause her husband found someone better?

BENJAMIN. Uh... I mean, it's complicated, but...

TREY. *(Re: the TV show.)* The Jamaican guy is so funny in this.

(In a horrible Jamaican accent.) Yeah mon, yeah!

BENJAMIN. Where do you, like, come from?

TREY. Oh I'm from Oklahoma. Okie boy here! What what!!!

BENJAMIN. Is that where you met Elliot?

TREY. Nah, we met in Florida.

BENJAMIN. What were you, why were you in Florida?

TREY. Yeah. We met in Florida. Yeah. And then... what the, what's like that thing people say, like, it's history, or –

BENJAMIN. The rest is hist–

TREY. Yeah. It's history.

BENJAMIN. And now what do you do?

TREY. Live here.

BENJAMIN. No but what do you do for work?

TREY. What is it with the people in this family? Everyone's, like, obsessed with work.

I'm pursuing some things. I'm trying to start this exercise line –

BENJAMIN. But, I mean, how much does that pay? Or are you, just, like, are you just living off of Elliot's money? Like, completely.

TREY. I don't know, how much does it pay to do whatever the fuck you're doing in, what, your fucking study fags abroad.

BENJAMIN. I'm in college. I'm taking classes.

TREY. Uh huh, and who pays for that?

BENJAMIN. My parents. My mom, mostly.

TREY. So there you go.

BENJAMIN. Uh, my mom's earned her money, she's a lawyer, she's at, like one of the biggest firms in LA –

TREY. Yeah but how'd she get to be a lawyer?

BENJAMIN. What?

TREY. Offa Elliot's money. He paid for everything, right?

BENJAMIN. Yeah but that's his daughter.

TREY. And I bet you got a trust fund, too, don't ya?

BENJAMIN. I'm his grandson.

TREY. So?

BENJAMIN. So I was born into the family, it's my right to, to like...

TREY. To what?

BENJAMIN. To have it.

TREY. Oh hell no, nobody just has the right to that much money.

BENJAMIN. He earned it. My family came from nothing. We had nothing.

TREY. Well you don't got nothing no more, do you?

BENJAMIN. So you just, like, you just want Elliot's money?

TREY. *(With absolute sincerity.)* What? Dude. No. I'm his partner.

BENJAMIN. But are you like, are you even attracted to him?

TREY. Dude. I'm his partner.

BENJAMIN. Are you even gay?

TREY. What?

BENJAMIN. Are you gay?

TREY. I don't do labels man...

BENJAMIN. So how do you identify? What are you?

TREY. I'm not anything. I'm just Trey.

BENJAMIN. Right but like, are you attracted to men more, or women?

TREY. I just care about the person inside, and El's a good person, so it's good.

BENJAMIN. I'm sorry, but no one cares about the person inside. Well, men don't. Do you like being with men?

(**TREY** *looks over at* **BENJAMIN** *with a smile.*)

TREY. Why are you so curious?

BENJAMIN. What? I'm just... I'm curious.

TREY. I like spending good time with good people.

BENJAMIN. So do you still like women too?

TREY. Hell yeah I like women. Hellllllll yeah.

BENJAMIN. Ok.

TREY. And I still fuck – El doesn't have a problem with that – I still fuck chicks. El does too. I mean, not anymore, but he did, so, he gets it.

BENJAMIN. But, like, ok I – can I ask, do you... do you like having sex? With Elliot?

TREY. I mean – what do you want me to say? It's definitely too much for me – that thing is a fuckin' JAWBREAKER.

BENJAMIN. Oh I don't want to –

TREY. But apparently that's like a family tradition or something?

BENJAMIN. What is?

TREY. Huge fucking dicks. He said his dad had a huge one too. I always thought I was big, but Elliot's like – but I guess that's a family thing.

BENJAMIN. It is?

TREY. I mean – you tell me.

BENJAMIN. Oh.

> (**BENJAMIN** *is not hung. Not even a little. And in the last twenty minutes he's learned that his father is, and his grandfather, and his great-grandfather, and he's feeling really weird.*)

TREY. Don't feel bad. It don't matter, really...

Here's the thing, man: relationships is work. And, I'll shoot straight with you – El is suuuuper controlling, and everything, like, if he even sees me talking to someone else I gotta listen to a lecture about it for two days, but like, my life, is so much better since I met El. Like, everything in my life is better. So that's what matters, you know? That's all that matters.

> (*Beat.*)

BENJAMIN. What was your life like before you met my grandpa?

TREY. Shitty man.

Or, not shitty, but, rough. Really rough.

BENJAMIN. Huh.

TREY. I mean, ain't no one ever took me to Italy 'fore I met El. That was frickin awesome. Dude. You ever been to Venice?

BENJAMIN. It's a tourist trap.

TREY. What? Dude, no. Venice is awesome. I rode a gondola, and I got a really cool photo of me in that square, with all the pigeons? El did let me do that, so, that was cool.

BENJAMIN. Well don't get too attached.

TREY. To what?

BENJAMIN. Venice. It's gonna sink. In our lifetime, probably.

TREY. Are you serious?

BENJAMIN. Yeah. Welcome to the twenty-first century.

TREY. Shit, man.

BENJAMIN. Yeah. But, Florence is better anyway.

TREY. Oh yeah? You like the Uffizi?

> (**BENJAMIN** *is genuinely surprised and impressed that* **TREY** *knows what the Uffizi is.*)

BENJAMIN. I like the David.

TREY. Course you do! You like that ass!

BENJAMIN. I mean... I guess – what?

TREY. Naw man, I'm just messin' with you. The David was way cooler than I thought cause I had this guidebook, we went everywhere it said, mostly churches and shit, and most places you just show up, take a picture and move on, but the David was different cause for some reason it's like impossible to just take a picture and go, it's like a magnet, it pulls you in, like, physically, and then you see it happen to all these tourist fucks, there's this long hallway and you can see their faces change as they get closer, like there's something in their bones or something, like, they can't walk away, cause they can't deny the power of like... I don't even know.

BENJAMIN. Beauty?

TREY. Maybe, yeah.

BENJAMIN. They come from all over the world to see a statue a gay guy made of a nice Jewish boy. Makes you think the world isn't such a bad place after all.

> (*Beat.* **TREY** *watches TV.* **BENJAMIN** *stares at* **TREY.** *At his face.*)

TREY. What dude?

BENJAMIN. What? Oh, nothing.

TREY. You're staring at me, like...

BENJAMIN. No, I just, I've never really met someone like you before.

TREY. In what respect?

BENJAMIN. Um, like, in all respects.

TREY. Awww. You're sweet.

I'm glad you ain't like your momma.

We should go riding tomorrow!

BENJAMIN. Riding?

TREY. Yeah man. Motorcycles. It's freaking so cool. I'll take you tomorrow.

BENJAMIN. Is it safe?

TREY. Yeah. I take El all the time. It's totally safe.

BENJAMIN. Isn't he a little old for that?

TREY. No, he does good. Age is just a number, anyway.

BENJAMIN. Um, not really, actually. Like, like even just someone's hands, he has the hands of a seventy-year-old, you know? I'm twenty. Mine are a lot nicer. Because I'm twenty. Because age isn't just a number.

TREY. Let me see.

(BENJAMIN *shows* TREY *his hand.*)

Yeah you do have nice hands.

I got some scars on this hand, from when I went riding once, got a little banged up, but, I think it's part of my charm, like, like everyone's bodies just tell a story about like, like about their whole life, you know? It's crazy. Cause see this?

(*He holds out his leg, points to a spot on his upper thigh.*)

See that?

BENJAMIN. Yeah.

TREY. That's from when I was seven, me and my brother were at this weird like pond like thing, it wasn't really a pond but people swum there, and like, one time me and my brother was just goofing around, and then outta nowhere this snake comes out and bites me, right there, and left that mark.

BENJAMIN. Wow.

TREY. Yeah. So it's like, my whole body just has a lot of stories, like, all over it.

BENJAMIN. I don't have that many scars. Just this one, on the back of my arm, it's small now.

TREY. Yeah I can't barely see it. How'd you get it?

BENJAMIN. I was, in high school, my gym locker was near this group of guys I was sort of obsessed with, one day we were changing and one of them actually talked to me, so my heart was like a mile a minute, but I was trying to play it cool – but I was like standing against the frame and I didn't realize my arm was in it, I basically slammed my own locker on my arm.

TREY. Ow.

BENJAMIN. Yeah. It was bleeding and everything.

TREY. Oh man.

BENJAMIN. Yeah but it was kinda worth it, he got paper towels and wrapped it for me, cause I couldn't really reach. And he was just in his underwear the whole time, so that was cool.

TREY. Ha.

BENJAMIN. I used to feel so tortured around those guys, cause they were so hot, but then like their dads, would show up, for a school function or whatever and they'd be... hideous. Weird thinning hairlines and like German Shepherd wrists and hairy knuckles, and these spongy asses. There were a couple dads who still had waistlines or jawlines but you could tell they had to work so hard to maintain them, and knowing the effort they put in just to not look totally gross somehow made them even grosser than the ones who just let themselves go. And then I'd turn back to look at their sons who I was obsessed with and it would be like, oh! Right! The only reason you're attractive is because your youth is like Chernobyling out of you right now, but in thirty years you're gonna be like your dads, which is, you know, not cute, and once I realized that, I felt a million times less depressed, and even by the time I graduated, a couple of the guys who'd been like so sexy to me in ninth or tenth grade were already starting to go into decline, and that's how I knew I'd, like, survive.

But like, the idea of sleeping with one of those dads makes me almost sick to my stomach, and sleeping with someone who's seventy is like...

(Beat. **TREY** *smiles.)*

Can I see it again? The snake bite?

(A long beat. Then, **BENJAMIN** *touches it.)*

TREY. Weird, right?

BENJAMIN. Yeah.

> *(He is more than touching* **TREY**'s *leg now. And* **TREY** *is kind of letting him.* **BENJAMIN** *looks at* **TREY**'s *face.* **TREY** *stares straight ahead, watching TV.* **BENJAMIN** *is about to lean in when –)*

ELLIOT. Time for bed, Trey.

> *(***ELLIOT**, *in a bathrobe, stands on the stairs. He'd been obscured by darkness. We don't know he's there until he speaks, and we don't know how long he's been listening.* **BENJAMIN** *freezes.* **TREY**, *unfazed, finishes the gallon of milk.)*

TREY. *(Under his breath.)* Housed that.

(He wipes his mouth with the back of his hand, puts the empty bottle on the table, throws the shirt back toward Benjamin, and goes upstairs to **ELLIOT***, who waits for him, as* **BENJAMIN** *stares at the TV.)*

(Blackout.)

ACT II

Scene One

(The next morning. An empty living room. **JODI** *enters from the kitchen, holding a cup of coffee. She walks over to the couch, sits down, then remembers that Trey sat on it bare-assed, stands up, and walks away.)*

*(**ORSOLYA** comes downstairs.)*

JODI. Good morning.

ORSOLYA. Good morning.

JODI. Excuse me, have you seen my dad?

ORSOLYA. He's upstairs with the doctor.

JODI. The doctor?

ORSOLYA. He just, small procedure.

JODI. What?

(She goes to the bottom of the stairs. **JEFF** *enters with flowers, which he arranges.* **ORSOLYA** *exits.)*

Daddy?

Daddy?

ELLIOT. *(Offstage.)* Just a second.

*(**JODI** turns and admires the flowers **JEFF** has placed on the table.)*

JODI. He always has the most beautiful flowers.

JEFF. He does.

JODI. I wish Daddy was as thoughtful about picking men as he is about picking flowers.

JEFF. Well. He certainly likes everything to be fresh.

JODI. How long do you give them? Another month? Two?

>   *(Quick beat.)*

JEFF. When they're out, walking, in public... Elliot holds
    Trey's hand.

JODI. Ok...

JEFF. He's never done that before. Not with anyone.

>   *(He exits as* **ELLIOT** *descends the stairs, an ice
>   pack pressed against his face.)*

JODI. Daddy! What happened?

ELLIOT. Nothing. But I need to talk with you –

JODI. Are you ok? You saw a doctor?

ELLIOT. I just had a little...

JODI. A little what?

ELLIOT. A little – filler. But I need to talk with you –

JODI. On your birthday? You're so crazy, Daddy. Happy
    Birthday by the – let me see what you did to your –

>   *(She removes the ice pack.)*

>   You're all swollen.

ELLIOT. I just had it done, it goes down fast.

JODI. Botox on your birthday?

ELLIOT. She's still upstairs, if you want?

JODI. No. I'm – Why? Do you think I need something done?
    Say no.

ELLIOT. No.

JODI. Thank you.

ELLIOT. Uh huh. Listen, we need to –

JODI. You know, Daddy, you look so great when you're, you
    know, natural. It's such an awesome look for you –

ELLIOT. Jodi?

JODI. You didn't ask my opinion, I know –

ELLIOT. *(On "ask my.")* I didn't ask your opinion but that's
    not what I'm trying to say. I need to talk to you.

JODI. So talk, who's stopping you?

ELLIOT. You need to keep your son in check.

JODI. Excuse me?

ELLIOT. What's not clear about that? You need to keep your son in check.

> (**ORSOLYA** *walks through with a huge laundry basket full of Benjamin's clean clothes. She takes them upstairs.)*

JODI. What's wrong with my son?

ELLIOT. He needs to remember he is a guest in this house.

JODI. You've gone out of your way to make sure he feels that way, don't worry.

ELLIOT. Excuse me?

JODI. Maybe you could spend a little time with him? Take an interest in him?

ELLIOT. That's not our issue here.

JODI. Then what's our issue?

ELLIOT. Your son would do well to remember that Trey is with *me*.

JODI. Ew. What?

ELLIOT. Your son would do well to remember that Trey. Is with. Me.

JODI. Well your *partner* would do well to remember that it's inappropriate to walk around the house butt naked when your *grandson* is here.

ELLIOT. And I am dealing with that, believe me.

JODI. I hope you are! Maybe you should think about how confusing it is for a twenty-year-old when his grandfather's NAKED BOYFRIEND walks around in front of him. Who's also twenty! Of course they want to... hang out, that's how twenty-year-olds are, they do twenty-year-old things with other twenty-year-olds. They don't hang out with *seventy*-year-old men I'm sorry but they don't and, people are laughing at you.

ELLIOT. No one is laughing at me.

JODI. They are, Daddy. I – I know you hate it when I google you, and I almost never do, but –

ELLIOT. Uh huh.

JODI. But, people are laughing at you. Online.

ELLIOT. Ok.

JODI. You're like, the laughingstock of the internet right now.

ELLIOT. So what?

>   *(Beat.)*

How so?

JODI. Oh Daddy, the two of you make a, uh, it's quite a pair, let's put it that way. I'm not trying to be... unkind, but, how well do you really know this guy?

>   *(**ELLIOT** says nothing.)*

Have fun, no one wants you to have fun more than I do, but I am the most important person in your life. And I am telling you to be careful.

>   *(**TREY** appears. He's tentative. He also has an ice pack on his face. **ELLIOT** turns away.)*

You, too?

TREY. What?

JODI. *You* had botox?

TREY. So?

JODI. You're twenty!

TREY. *(Duh.) Preventative* botox.

JODI. Ok then. Well. Nice to see you. In clothing. It's a good look for you.

TREY. Thanks? Babes? You – you ready?

>   *(**ELLIOT** ignores **TREY**.)*

JODI. Where you going, birthday boy?

TREY. It's a surprise.

JODI. Daddy hates surprises.

TREY. But – it's for your birthday.

>   *(Quick beat.)*

El?

JODI. It doesn't look like *El* is up for any more surprises.

TREY. But, I… I booked us massages. For your birthday. So, will you come on?

JODI. Why don't they just come here?

TREY. Cause we get the seaweed wraps, but they stink up the house, can't do that here.

(Upstairs, we hear **ORSOLYA** and **BENJAMIN**.)

ORSOLYA. (Offstage.) I left your clothes outside your door.

BENJAMIN. (Offstage.) I saw, thank you.

TREY. Babes?

ORSOLYA. (Offstage.) You're welcome.

TREY. Car's out front, so…

(**BENJAMIN** enters and comes downstairs.)

JODI. Good morning.

BENJAMIN. Hi.

JODI. How'd you sleep?

BENJAMIN. Ok.

(Beat.)

JODI. Benji. Is there something you want to say?

BENJAMIN. What?

JODI. To Elliot.

BENJAMIN. Uhm, what?

JODI. About… today?

BENJAMIN. Oh. Happy Birthday.

ELLIOT. Ok.

TREY. Babes? Wanna hit the road?

BENJAMIN. Where you going?

TREY. We're getting seaweed wraps.

BENJAMIN. I thought we were going riding?

JODI. Riding?

BENJAMIN. Motorcycles.

JODI. No no no no no. We are not riding motorcycles.

BENJAMIN. You said, you were gonna take me…

(**BENJAMIN** *looks at* **TREY**. **ELLIOT** *does too.*)

TREY. Yeah. Just, I meant, like, sometime. I didn't know you meant, like, today.

BENJAMIN. I mean, I'm not here, like, ever. So... Today's the only day I can really go. So...

TREY. Next time.

BENJAMIN. But –

TREY. Sorry dude.

BENJAMIN. But, but –

ELLIOT. *(Intense.)* You heard him, Benjamin. When people say no it means no.

(**BENJAMIN** *is taken aback.* **ELLIOT** *stands up.*)

Shall we?

(*He extends his hand.* **TREY** *comes, stands beside* **ELLIOT**, *and holds it. When* **BENJAMIN** *sees this, he runs upstairs. Then* **ELLIOT** *and* **TREY** *exit.* **JODI***'s alone. Again. She calls upstairs:*)

JODI. BENJAMIN!

BENJAMIN MICHAEL ISAAC CULLEN!!!

BENJAMIN. *(Offstage.)* WHAT?

JODI. I need to speak with you!

BENJAMIN. *(Offstage.)* No.

JODI. GET DOWN HERE NOW!

BENJAMIN. *(Offstage.)* WHAT?

JODI. NOW!

(**BENJAMIN** *comes to the top of the stairs.*)

BENJAMIN. What?

JODI. You can't fuck your grandfather's boyfriend, is that clear?

BENJAMIN. I didn't fuck anybody!

JODI. Don't walk away from me when I'm talking to you. You cannot fuck Trey. Got it?

BENJAMIN. Mom, stop.

(**JEFF** *walks through the room.*)

JODI. I get that it's confusing, he's your age, he's walking around with his ass hanging out, he's –

BENJAMIN. Mom.

JODI. He has that body, great body, and he's –

BENJAMIN. Mom!

JODI. Very attractive, but –

BENJAMIN. Stop!

JODI. But at the end of the day, he's with Daddy. For now. So, hands off.

BENJAMIN. I didn't even do anything!

JODI. I'm not done with you.

(**BENJAMIN** *trudges downstairs.*)

BENJAMIN. What?

JODI. Tell me what happened last night.

BENJAMIN. Nothing!

JODI. You two were down here for a while, I could hear it.

BENJAMIN. You were eavesdropping on me? Nice.

JODI. I wasn't – What'd you talk about?

BENJAMIN. If you heard, you know.

JODI. I didn't hear words – I wasn't trying to listen. But you were down here for a long time, so tell me.

BENJAMIN. Tell you what?

JODI. What'd you find out? What's his deal?

BENJAMIN. He doesn't have a deal. He's from Oklahoma.

JODI. Did you find out any more about *Bryce*?

BENJAMIN. No.

JODI. What about Daddy's money? Did he say anything about –

BENJAMIN. No.

JODI. Come on Benji! Give me something!

BENJAMIN. He said Elliot's got a huge dick.

JODI. Oh. That's not what I –

BENJAMIN. I believe his exact words were "jawbreaker."

JODI. Ok I did not need to know that.

BENJAMIN. But, that was it.

JODI. Ok.

BENJAMIN. He's actually pretty nice, once you get to know him –

JODI. Benjamin! No. Do not start disappointing me as a human being. N. O.

BENJAMIN. But one-on-one he really is –

JODI. N. O. Can't handle it. Got it? NO.

BENJAMIN. Can I go now?

JODI. No. What do you want to do with me today?

BENJAMIN. Nothing.

JODI. Benjamin I haven't seen you in months, you can do something with ME. With your mother. With the normal people. You want to visit Grandma Sylvia?

BENJAMIN. Not really.

JODI. Great, then why don't we do that. You can Yiddish with her.

BENJAMIN. She's comatose.

JODI. You can still practice.

BENJAMIN. I DON'T SPEAK YIDDISH!

JODI. Well you speak English? Go get dressed.

(**BENJAMIN** *begins walking upstairs.*)

BENJAMIN. This is so stupid.

JODI. I know. The whole world is so stupid. Life is so stupid. Go get dressed. We're having mother-son time.

BENJAMIN. I'd rather die.

JODI. Maybe I'd rather die too, did you ever think about that? Now go get dressed.

(**BENJAMIN**'*s gone.* **ORSOLYA** *comes downstairs with an ice pack on her forehead.*)

You're kidding, right?

ORSOLYA. She's packing up, if you want anything before she goes?

JODI. No. I don't. The lines on your face – that's your history. I don't want to erase my history. And besides, I don't need it.

Scene Two

(*Later that night.*)

(**JEFF** *enters with a platter of hors d'oeuvres, places them on the table, then exits. He returns with a second platter. He takes his time arranging items.*)

(*On the other side of the stage, quietly,* **ELLIOT** *emerges in a dark suit, white shirt, no tie.* **JEFF** *doesn't know he's there.* **ELLIOT** *stares at* **JEFF**, *taking him in, watching him bent over the table.*)

(*As this happens,* **BENJAMIN** *appears, looking nice. No one notices him. He watches* **ELLIOT** *watching* **JEFF**.)

(*After a long beat,* **JEFF** *can feel a pair of eyes burning a hole through him. He freezes, turns around, sees* **ELLIOT** *staring, then spots* **BENJAMIN**. **ELLIOT** *turns to see* **BENJAMIN**, *too.*)

JEFF. Can I get you something to drink?

ELLIOT. Pellegrino.

BENJAMIN. Can I just have a Diet Coke?

ELLIOT. Thank you Jeff.

(**JEFF** *exits.* **BENJAMIN** *comes downstairs.*)

BENJAMIN. Where's Mom?

ELLIOT. Upstairs changing.

BENJAMIN. Where's Trey?

(**ELLIOT** *turns to look at him.*)

ELLIOT. Changing.

BENJAMIN. How's your birthday going so far?

ELLIOT. Very nice thank you.

This one is gluten-free.

BENJAMIN. Oh. Thanks.

ELLIOT. When do you fly back to Budapest?

BENJAMIN. Tomorrow night.

ELLIOT. Uh huh. And you're there until…

BENJAMIN. Like another two months.

ELLIOT. Ok, well, I just asked you two questions, so before you go whining to your mommy that no one takes an interest in you here, think twice.

> (**JODI** *descends the stairs, wearing a very pretty dress, almost girlish, not seductive. She's clearly made an effort to look beautiful.*)

JODI. Hey party boys.

> (*No one looks at her, or comments on her dress. She approaches* **BENJAMIN.**)

Don't you look handsome. Is there enough for you to eat?

ELLIOT. We have some gluten-free.

JODI. Oh good. Have you been in the kitchen?

ELLIOT. Yes.

JODI. And? Did you see what they were making?

ELLIOT. I saw they were cooking…

JODI. No but did you see what it was?

ELLIOT. … Chicken?

JODI. Chicken paillard.

ELLIOT. Ok. Great.

JODI. Daddy! Chicken *paillard*!

ELLIOT. Yes, you said.

BENJAMIN. He doesn't remember.

ELLIOT. Remember what?

JODI. Nothing. Forget it.

ELLIOT. Remember what?

JODI. Nothing.

BENJAMIN. Oh Mom. Elliot asked me two questions. He's taking an interest.

JODI. Isn't that nice? Did you show him how you do Yiddish? He does know a little bit, it's so adorable.

BENJAMIN. No, we talked about this, remember? I'm a person, not a monkey.

JODI. But did you show Daddy your pictures from Budapest? Who knew it was so stunning, I don't know why our family left.

BENJAMIN. Uhm...

JODI. He went to a Holocaust memorial. Did you tell Daddy?

BENJAMIN. No.

JODI. Tell him.

BENJAMIN. Mom.

JODI. Tell him.

BENJAMIN. I went to a Holocaust memorial.

JODI. He looked for our family.

BENJAMIN. Itzakovak, right? That's what it was, before you changed it?

ELLIOT. Itzakovich.

BENJAMIN. Itzakovich, right. Well, I found like six people with that name, so I guess our family didn't all get out in time.

JODI. Wow. I mean, history, right?

> (**TREY** *descends the staircase. He's in a tuxedo. He is stunning. Everyone turns to stare. They can't help themselves.*)

ELLIOT. Wow.

TREY. You said to look nice, so...

JODI. I didn't say black tie. I said nice.

> (**JEFF** *returns with* **ELLIOT** *and* **BENJAMIN**'s *drinks.*)

ELLIOT. It fits perfectly.

TREY. It's a little tight in the... *(Unspoken: crotch.)*

ELLIOT. No. It fits...

JEFF. Ma'am, would you like a drink?

JODI. Ma'am? Yeah, definitely.

JEFF. What would you like?

JODI. I don't know. Something with alcohol. What do you have? Pinot grigio.

(**JEFF** *exits.*)

ELLIOT. It fits perfectly.

TREY. Get me a beer!

(**ELLIOT** *takes in* **TREY** *for a beat.*)

JODI. I feel like maybe my dress is a little big. Maybe I should have had it taken in a little maybe.

ELLIOT. What? No, you look nice.

TREY. Yeah, cool dress.

JODI. You don't have to say I look nice if you don't think I look nice, I wasn't fishing for compliments. I was genuinely like, not sure about the fit. That's all.

ELLIOT. You look lovely.

JODI. But you don't have to say that! I didn't make the dress, I legitimately like, do not care if you like my *dress* or not.

ELLIOT. But you look beautiful, Jodi. You really do.

JODI. But that's what I'm saying. Who cares if I look beautiful? It. Doesn't. Matter. It's fleeting. Going, going, gone. Young, gorgeous, gone. Helen of Troy is completely gone. That's how it works. I'm just glad I got my degree, went to law school, made something of myself. Of my *mind*. A degree is forever. Your mind, that's forever. That's what counts.

(*Tapping her brain.*) *This* is what counts.

(*To* **BENJAMIN**.) I need you to remember that, ok?

TREY. You're acting really weird, lady.

JODI. Well, it's been a really weird day.

BENJAMIN. We visited Grandma Sylvia.

ELLIOT. I told you not to visit Mom.

JODI. You were right, ok?

ELLIOT. What happened? Did she talk?

JODI.	**BENJAMIN.**
Not really –	Oh she talked.

ELLIOT. Oh?

BENJAMIN. Yeah. I was like, Grandma Sylvia, vos makhstu –
that's Yiddish for wassup – and she looked me dead in
the eye and called me: faygele. Over and over and over.

JODI. She didn't know what she was saying.

BENJAMIN. Mmm, I think she did.

TREY. What's faygele?

ELLIOT. It means little bird.

TREY. Why would she call you a little bird?

BENJAMIN. Because it means faggot.

JODI. Benji, I hate that –

BENJAMIN. That's what it means.

TREY. Your grandma called you a faggot?

BENJAMIN. My great-grandma. Multiple times. In Yiddish.

(**TREY** *can't stop laughing.*)

ELLIOT. Trey.

I told you not to go see her.

JODI. You said she was comatose.

ELLIOT. She usually is.

BENJAMIN. She said a couple other things, but I couldn't
understand.

JODI. Don't worry honey. I'm sure whatever it was, it wasn't
important. Or else it was incredibly unkind.

BENJAMIN. She told Mom that she was –

JODI. Benji!! You know what? We don't need to share
everything, ok? Let's – Trey? Would you? I need some
pictures with my family.

TREY. What?

(**JODI** *gives* **TREY** *her phone.*)

JODI. Will you take our picture? Benji? Daddy? Let's all get
together, uhm, over here.

(**ELLIOT** *and* **BENJAMIN** *make their way to*
JODI.)

That's good. Ok, everyone looks so nice. Let's, uhm, yeah, ok.

(**ELLIOT** and **BENJAMIN** *flank her.*)

TREY. One, two, three.

JODI. Take one more. So we have options.

TREY. One, two, three.

JODI. Let me see.

Aww. These are sweet. Aren't these sweet?

(**ELLIOT** *looks.*)

ELLIOT. Do it again, Trey. Over here.

(*He points* **TREY** *toward a different light.*)

TREY. Better?

ELLIOT. I don't know, take the picture first.

TREY. One, two, three. You want options?

JODI. Yeah, thanks.

TREY. Ok. One, two, three. Oh these are good.

JODI. Oh thanks. Can I... Trey –

TREY. Hang on.

(*He exits with* **JODI**'s *phone.*)

JODI. Trey, can I have my...

(*Beat.* **JODI** *is exhausted at the thought of having to chase* **TREY** *for her phone.*)

Daddy can you help me get my...

(*She sighs, then stands to go get* **TREY**. *Before she gets too far, he returns with* **ORSOLYA**.)

TREY. Ok, let's all get together. Take a couple, so we got options. Everyone say cheese!

JODI. What? Oh...

(**TREY** *gets between* **ELLIOT** *and* **BENJAMIN**, *forcing* **JODI** *to be on the end next to* **BENJAMIN**.)

(**ORSOLYA** *snaps some photos. She's almost emotional.*)

ORSOLYA. Gorgeous. Gorgeous family.

JODI. Uhm. That's...

> (**ORSOLYA** *gives the phone back to* **TREY** *and exits.*)

Trey, can I have my –

TREY. Oh these are awesome. Hell yeah.

JODI. Can I have my...

TREY. El, look at us.

> (*He is sort of cuddled into* **ELLIOT**, *who has his arm around him.*)

Will you send these to me?

JODI. Can I have my phone?

> (**TREY** *passes the phone back to* **JODI.** **TREY** *and* **ELLIOT** *are cuddled together.* **JODI** *and* **BENJAMIN** *look at them for a long time.*)

I have to...

I need to, uhm...

I think it's time for presents. Benji? You wanna come help me get my present? I left it in Antony's office.

> (**BENJAMIN** *can't stop watching* **TREY** *with* **ELLIOT**.)

BENJAMIN. My present's upstairs.

JODI. What?

BENJAMIN. My present's upstairs.

JODI. You got Daddy your own present? That is so thoughtful. I'm... blown away...

> (*Quick beat.*)

TREY. I – I already gave you my present.

JODI. You did?

TREY. Yeah, we got seaweed wraps.

JODI. You bought those?

ELLIOT. That's alright.

TREY. It was my idea, and I'm the one who tole Antony to book 'em, so...

JODI. So you don't have any present?

Huh.

TREY. I planned those massages...

(**JODI** *exits.* **BENJAMIN** *goes upstairs.*)

I thought the massages would be a cool present. I didn't know everyone was doing, like, whatever.

ELLIOT. I don't even like presents.

TREY. But I totally planned those massages!

This party sucks. You wanna get outta here? We could go to the Boom Boom Room. We could go dancing...

(**JEFF** *enters with drinks.* **TREY** *sees him.*)

Dude. You'd be so good delivering pizzas.

ELLIOT. Trey.

TREY. Nah but look how good he is! It's a skill. I'd love to see what you can do with, like, six pizzas.

ELLIOT. Please. Be good.

TREY. Course, babes.

(**JEFF** *holds* **TREY**'s *drink. There are many things he'd like to do with it, but finally he places it on a coaster. As he's doing so,* **TREY** *calls out in the style of Little Caesars:*)

Pizza! Pizza!

ELLIOT. TREY!

(*This is intense.* **ELLIOT** *rises.* **TREY** *is still.*)

Thank you Jeff. I'm – I'm sorry.

(**JEFF**'s *face says, "I'm sorry too. For you." But he says nothing, and exits. Then* **ELLIOT** *turns, his back to the audience, staring at* **TREY**.*)

TREY. Why are you looking at me like that?

You're scaring me.

El?

(Before **ELLIOT** *can respond, he sees* **BENJAMIN** *standing at the top of the stairs. Upon being noticed,* **BENJAMIN** *comes downstairs.)*

BENJAMIN. Hey, so... I didn't get a chance to wrap it, but...

ELLIOT. Should we wait for your mom?

JODI. *(Offstage.)* I'm right here.

(She returns, carrying a square-shaped box.)

BENJAMIN. I was just saying, I didn't get a chance to wrap it.

JODI. It's the thought that counts, honey.

BENJAMIN. Ok, well then, Happy Birthday.

(He hands **ELLIOT** *a book.)*

ELLIOT. Horatio Alger.

BENJAMIN. I figured, everyone's called you the Horatio Alger of Brooklyn long enough, you should know about your namesake.

JODI. Wow is that thoughtful!

ELLIOT. *Ragged Dick*?

BENJAMIN. Yeah it's his most famous book. Horatio Alger wrote all these rags-to-riches stories, that's how the myth sort of –

ELLIOT. It's underlined.

BENJAMIN. Well, it's kinda my copy, but... I think you'll like it. We read it in queer studies.

ELLIOT. Well great. Thank you.

TREY. *Ragged Dick*?

BENJAMIN. Yeah. It's about a boy who goes from rags to riches but the thing is, no one just *goes* to riches, what *actually* happens is, this poor boy meets a much older, wealthy, worldly gentleman who takes an interest in him, of a sexual nature, and then, well... the rest is history.

JODI. Sounds like a great read.

ELLIOT. Thank you.

BENJAMIN. You're welcome.

JODI. Ok. My turn. So. Daddy. From Benji and Grayson and me: we want to wish you a very, very Happy Birthday.

(**ELLIOT** *opens the box and takes out an album.*)

ELLIOT. What is this?

JODI. It's photos, from your whole life. From before you were born, until –

(**ELLIOT** *opens the album.*)

ELLIOT. Oh god, those are my grandparents, Jacob and Lena.

JODI. Daddy was very close to Grandma Lena.

ELLIOT. She used to tell everyone we were related to Leslie Howard.

JODI. Right!

(*At some point,* **TREY** *begins to make his way to* **ELLIOT**.)

BENJAMIN. Who's that?

ELLIOT. A movie star. From the '30s.

JODI. *Gone With the Wind*? Oh come on, Benji.

BENJAMIN. I mean, I've heard of it.

JODI. Ashley Wilkes? What kind of gay are you? Although I thought he was British?

ELLIOT. Who, Leslie Howard? His father was a Hungarian Jew. At least, according to Lena.

JODI. And Grandpa was a tailor. So you see? It's all in the DNA.

TREY. Who's that?

JODI. That's Grandma Sylvia. At her wedding.

ELLIOT. Wow.

BENJAMIN. She does not look like that anymore.

JODI. Well, that's what happens if you stick around long enough.

TREY. Is that you?

ELLIOT. No, that's my brother.

TREY. Where's he?

ELLIOT. He's dead. That's me.

TREY. Is that where you grew up?

ELLIOT. Uh huh.

TREY. Wow. You was like, you was as poor as I used to be.

ELLIOT. Oh we had nothing. Grandma Lena used to come with an oversized purse and try and sneak bread into our bread basket, but my mother was so proud she would throw it away.

JODI. This is Daddy with his first Singer sewing machine.

ELLIOT. The other boys were outside playing stickball. I was inside sewing.

BENJAMIN. And you had no idea you were attracted to men?

JODI. Here's your Bar Mitzvah. High school graduation. Here's his wedding to Mommy. She was so beautiful.

TREY. Where is she?

JODI. She died, fifteen years ago, now. Breast cancer.

BENJAMIN. Is that...

ELLIOT. That's the first store we ever opened, on 56th Street.

JODI. Look at Grandma Sylvia, cutting the ribbon. Has a person ever looked happier, anywhere on Earth?

TREY. Dude. You were smokin'!

JODI. He still is.

TREY. Yeah but...

JODI. There's me.

BENJAMIN. Is that when you lived in Brooklyn?

JODI. No, I think they'd left by then, right?

ELLIOT. We left Brooklyn when you were two.

JODI. So then that has to still be Brooklyn.

ELLIOT. That sounds right.

TREY. What are those pants?

JODI. It was the '70s.

ELLIOT. I'm proud to say, I didn't design those. But I did wear them.

JODI. Remember this?

ELLIOT. Oh, sure.

JODI. Mommy hit the roof when she saw this. I'm, what, nine? Ten?

ELLIOT. Something like that.

BENJAMIN. I can't believe you went to Studio 54.

JODI. Oh, I was like the Eloise of Studio 54.

TREY. What's Studio 54?

> (**JODI** *and* **ELLIOT** *smile at* **TREY**'s *question but don't answer it, and turn the page.*)

Who are those guys?

ELLIOT. Those were some of my friends – that's Brian. I don't recognize him. This guy's dead, this guy's probably dead. He's definitely dead. And he lives in Japan now.

JODI. Here's my Bat Mitzvah.

BENJAMIN. Your eyes look so glassy there.

> (*Pause.*)

ELLIOT. That was right before I... that was before.

> (*They turn two pages in silence.*)

TREY. Where's that?

ELLIOT. Mykonos. Greece.

TREY. That's frickin gorgeous.

ELLIOT. We'll go next summer.

TREY. Awesome!

JODI. Is that...

ELLIOT. Uh... yes. That's Jeff.

BENJAMIN. Like... Diet Coke Jeff?

> (*He points toward the kitchen.* **ELLIOT** *nods.*)

TREY. You went away together?

ELLIOT. A long time ago, a... long time ago.

JODI. Benji with Elliot. I love that picture.

All the way up to... five minutes ago!

ELLIOT. You –

JODI. I had Antony print it out just now. It's computer paper. We'll get it re-printed on photo stock, but I just wanted to celebrate, I'm only sorry Grayson couldn't be here.

TREY. You didn't use the picture with me.

(Quick beat.)

JODI. Oh, well, it's a family album.

ELLIOT. We'll have Antony print out the other photo.

TREY. Yeah.

JODI. Well, but, this is a family album, Daddy. It's about our family.

ELLIOT. Antony can print out the other photo.

TREY. I love you babes. Happy Birthday.

ELLIOT. Thank you.

*(It feels for a second like **ELLIOT**'s acting like **TREY** made this album for him. He and **TREY** kiss, for a while. **JODI** is fucking pissed.)*

JODI. It's from Benji and Grayson too.

ELLIOT. Thank you, sweetheart. This must have taken you days.

*(Conversation continues, but somehow **TREY** disappears during this, without anyone noticing.)*

JODI. It took a little time, but it's your – it's a big birthday, I wanted to recognize it.

*(**ORSOLYA** passes through the room.)*

It was fun actually, it brought back a lot of memories… I have to say though – Oh Orsolya – Benji, ask her – We, we found – we gave Daddy an album, for his birthday, and –

(She starts to take a photo out of the album.)

ORSOLYA. Very nice.

JODI. On the back of one of the photos, there was some writing, we didn't know what it said. It looks like…

BENJAMIN. I think it's Hungarian.

JODI. These are his grandparents, the ones from Hungary.

ORSOLYA. Oh yes. Very nice.

JODI. Can you tell us what it says?

ORSOLYA. Uhm, thank you for sending the photograph. It is good to see everyone looking well. It's been raining here, there has been so much rain. It was most unpleasant and Mother had a cold, but she is better now. It stopped raining.

> *(Quick beat.)*

JODI. Well. I'm glad that woman's cold got better.

> **(ORSOLYA** *begins to hand the photo back.)*

BENJAMIN. Can you read it in Hungarian?

JODI. You don't understand Hungarian, do you?

BENJAMIN. No. But I just want to hear it in Hungarian.

ORSOLYA. Köszönöm, hogy elküldte a fotográfiát. Örülök, hogy mindenki jól van. Itt sokat esett, nagyon sokat. Nagyon kellemetlen volt és Édesanya megfázott, de már jobban érzi magát. Már nem esik az eső.

> *(She hands the photo back, then exits. They are quiet, having heard a language their family once spoke, which none of them speak anymore.* **JODI** *puts the photo back in the album as* **TREY** *returns with an open bottle of champagne and four glasses. He pours champagne and passes out the glasses throughout the following.)*

ELLIOT. Oh, Trey, that's very sweet.

TREY. I know. I'm sweet.

So my present isn't like, a present. It's, more like a toast.

ELLIOT. Terrific.

JODI. Daddy.

ELLIOT. Yes?

JODI. You're not... You're not gonna drink that, are you?

ELLIOT. Do you see me drinking?

JODI. No, but –

ELLIOT. I'm allowed to comment on it.

TREY. You don't gotta drink it, it's just, you can't have a toast without something in it, is all. Right, babes?

ELLIOT. Absolutely.

JODI. Again. Trey. Going in the cellar and getting a bottle of champagne that someone else bought isn't the same as –

TREY. Ok so, can I have everyone's attention, please?

ELLIOT. Trey?

TREY. You be quiet. I'm making a toast.

JODI. Actually, *I* was going to make a toast –

TREY. You can make one at dinner.

JODI. But I was gonna make the first toast, Trey. That's actually, that's kind of important to me.

TREY. Ok. But I have a toast first. So just – you can go next.

JODI. But –

TREY. You can go next. Ok?

(*Quick beat.*)

Nervous.

ELLIOT. Aww.

TREY. Ok.

Breath.

Ok.

El. Babes. Donkey dick. That's a inside joke.

(*He takes a breath.*)

Ever since I met you, my life has been really good. Like, amazing good. And... I know we've had our ups, and I know we've had our downs, and all that stuff, and everything, but, I just want you to know I really love you.

JODI. Cheers.

TREY. And, you're like the most important person to me and everything, you know? And it's been so cool to meet Benjamin, and, cause he's so cool. And Jodi. And, uh, anyway, you know, I just wanted to say that.

JODI. Cheers.

TREY. So. I love you. And – like, I really do.

And, but, so the POINT of all this, is, like, I love you, so much, and everything, and like, with your family here the last day, it's just been like, it just feels really right to me, like, this is my family now, and like, you know, I don't ever want to lose you, because, I just don't, and I want us to be together forever and everything, and so, what I want to say is, is I wanna know will you marry me?

(Beat.)

Babes?

(Beat.)

JODI. Oh. That was so sweet. You really are a sweet kid, you are.

TREY. What are you –

JODI. Those were beautiful words you said about my daddy, they were.

TREY. El?

JODI. Daddy, this is mean. Say something.

TREY. El?

El?

ELLIOT. *(With absolute sincerity.)* Yes. I will marry you. Yes.

*(Over the course of these next lines, **JODI** and **BENJAMIN**, who had been sitting next to each other, move ever so slightly closer together, so their bodies are touching, connected during this uncertain moment.)*

TREY. Babes.

Babes I love you so much.

ELLIOT. I love you, too.

TREY. You shoulda seen the look on your face.

ELLIOT. I was... not expecting that! Not at all!

TREY. I know.

ELLIOT. When did you decide to do this?

TREY. I mean I think about it all the time. But like seeing how your life used to be, before all of this, I mean, I'm the same way, like, we come from the same place, except I'm from the Ozarks and you're from Brooklyn, but like, I just get you, and, you get me, and then, I mean, you're such a family guy family's like the most important thing to you so it just seemed right to do it while everyone's here, so...

ELLIOT. You are a marvel.

BENJAMIN. Ew. Is this for real?

     (Quick beat.)

JODI. No.

    Daddy's not marrying him, he's fucking him, there's a big difference.

ELLIOT. Jodi.

TREY. Why are you being mean?

JODI. *(In a bad Southern accent.)* I ain't bein' mean, I'm bein' real.

ELLIOT. Jodi.

TREY. This is the happiest day of my life, don't take that from me –

BENJAMIN. Oh shut the fuck up.

TREY. Dude! Show some fucking respect.

JODI. Don't tell my son to show *you* respect don't you *dare*!

TREY. Well no one asked *micropenis* over there to weigh in so –

BENJAMIN. Oh my god!

JODI. Excuse me???

ELLIOT. You told me nothing happened with you two, you told me –

TREY. I didn't! Nothing happened with us I tole you –

ELLIOT. Then how do you know he has a micro–

TREY. He told me! He told me his dick is tiny, I didn't see it!

BENJAMIN. Oh my god can everyone please stop talking about my please!

JODI. Yes this stops right now sweetie this stops right –

TREY. That's right Jodi's absolutely right, let's all be sweet we're a family now, we gotta be sweet –

JODI. No *we* are not a family, Trey, *you* are not in this family!

TREY. Yes I am I am now so you best get used to it!

JODI. You think you're special? You think you're fucking special?

ELLIOT. Enough!

JODI. You're a PIECE of ASS. You're a dick and two butt cheeks. That's all you are, that's all you'll ever be, BRYCE!

    (Quick beat.)

Did you think we weren't gonna find out about that? Well, you thought wrong. You want to be in this family? Well we don't really have PORN STARS in our family. No one in *this* family gets FUCKED for MONEY. The people in this family have a little thing called class, and dignity, and you don't have those things, which means, you will never, ever be in this family. Bryce. Never.

Did you know he did porn, Daddy?

ELLIOT. Of course I did.

JODI. And?

ELLIOT. And I could not be more proud of him than if he were my own child.

    *(**TREY** is emotional. It's strange to watch.)*

TREY. I just needed some money. I'm not a bad person I was just hungry.

ELLIOT. I know, I know, it's alright.

    *(Beat. **ELLIOT** waits until **TREY** is calm.)*

Sweetie?

JODI.	TREY.
Yes?	Yeah?

ELLIOT. *(To* **TREY.***)* Do me a favor? Take Benjamin, go upstairs and play Xbox.

I need to talk to Jodi.

TREY. Ok babes.

ELLIOT. Benjamin? That's my fiancé you're going upstairs with. Don't forget that.

> *(The boys leave.)*

JODI. What?

> *(***ELLIOT** *says nothing.)*

What?

ELLIOT. Just – I'm collecting my thoughts. Hang on.

JODI. Ok, well can I say something?

ELLIOT. No.

> *(He collects his thoughts.)*

I don't know what I did to make you hate me.

JODI. I don't hate you Daddy –

ELLIOT. Because I can't imagine, I can't conceive of why you would try to destroy my happiness.

JODI. I can't with your happiness, I just can't.

ELLIOT. I'm sorry you're unhappy, but I'm not. And I don't know why you would go out of your way to hurt me. When I have been about the most wonderful father any child could have.

JODI. Whoa whoa whoa. No, I'm sorry, but no. Mom raised me, you were barely around, and I've moved on from that and I've even forgiven you and we have a nice thing for the most part but let's not rewrite history.

ELLIOT. Jodi, maybe you need to go through that photo album again, but I was a wonderful father to you.

JODI. That is not why I made you that album.

ELLIOT. Then why else would you give me such a beautiful gift?

JODI. Daddy! You are going to marry this child? That's honestly what you want to do?

ELLIOT. Who am I hurting?

JODI. It's not about – you're being taken advantage of.

ELLIOT. How am I being taken advantage of?

JODI. He wants your money! That's the only reason he's with you!

ELLIOT. Is that what this is about? Money?

JODI. Certainly for him it is. Unless – I mean, you don't actually think he's attracted to you? You can't possibly believe that you arouse him, in the slightest.

ELLIOT. I guess I arouse him more than you aroused Greg.

JODI. Ouch.

ELLIOT. He makes me happy.

JODI. His dick makes you happy.

ELLIOT. Yes, it does.

JODI. Well that's not why Trey is with *you*. I can promise you that.

ELLIOT. Ok. So he likes my money. And I like him. And that's enough.

JODI. Jesus, Daddy. That's so sad.

ELLIOT. That's not sad. That's every relationship. That is every single relationship on the planet. It's just two people exchanging goods, it's about finding someone who has something you want, and you have something they want, and you exchange.

JODI. So it's purely physical, then.

ELLIOT. That's how it begins. That's how it begins for all people. And then other things come.

JODI. What else has come?

ELLIOT. How do you explain love?

JODI. Try.

ELLIOT. He's funny. He's fun. I have a good time with him. I feel more awake, when I'm around him, I feel awake. I feel more awake to my life.

JODI. Because he's beautiful –

ELLIOT. Yes, because he's beautiful.

JODI. Why is that so important?

　　　　(**ELLIOT**'s face says, "Because it is.")

And you think you're happier, you're more fulfilled being with Trey than some lovely like fifty-three-year-old lawyer, or businessman, or painter? Someone on your intellectual level, with a shared sense of history, someone who had achieved something – anything?

ELLIOT. I know I am.

JODI. Because he's hot.

ELLIOT. You really don't get it.

JODI. Get what? Hot?

ELLIOT. You say *hot* like it's this casual little – like it's nothing. Jodi: it's everything. *Hot* is everything. Look around you. This house – this life – has been paid for by hot. Hot is everything. It's everything.

JODI. What is so great about *hot*? Explain it to me! Explain it, because I don't get it. What is so great about hot?

ELLIOT. What is so great about hot?

Well.

For starters, in the morning. In the morning, I wake up, and the first thing I see is him. Lying next to me. I touch him. I touch his skin, that skin, stretched like a crisp, freshly-ironed sheet pulled tight across a perfectly made bed; creaseless; and all you want is to slip inside those sheets and stay there forever. When there's a vein, it doesn't get lost in a crevice or cavernous fold; it pushes up, right against the surface, the interior life throbbing right there, without the layers of fat and mottled skin and liver spots... you touch the chest, you can almost feel what's inside, so close. And here he stands, at twenty, just just *just* on the other side of it all, still dripping with the aftermath of having been made into something. Pulsing, pulsating, roaring American ingenuity. From the heartland. Cornfed. Who knows what cornfed even means, but the word is enough to just about stop my heart. Your mother and I made you almost fifty years ago; seven years ago, this boy had never even cum.

He has lived more years before puberty than he has since. He wakes up in the morning and he smells like sex. Do you know what a man my age smells like in the morning? After about thirty-five, you wake up and you really start to smell the stench of death on a person. By sixty, it's almost insufferable.

I want to wake up in the morning and smell sex. I want to taste it. I want to see it. I want to touch it. I want to feel it. Sex is life. It's manufacturing, making things, producing, invigorating, creating. Sex is life, it's life, and I want life. Because I love life. I love waking up next to him because it feels like life, and I love that, and I love him for it. I want to wake up next to life, Jodi. And I can. So why the fuck not?

(*Beat.*)

JODI. Ok. Ok. Fine. So you like beauty. You love his beauty. And that's enough for you. Fine. And you want to live with him? And lavish him with gifts, and give him all your money, and leave this house to him and everything in it? Fine. I can even accept that. But what I can't do, is I cannot sit here and listen to you say that you love him. Because what you just described, is *lust*. And I know the difference. I've spent my life living at the mercy of your lust. I learned the lesson so well I even married a man with the same... predilections. But lust is easy; love is hard. It's hard, to love your spouse, even your parents – it's so hard, they made it a commandment, next to murder and adultery.

There's no commandment to love your kid. That's supposed to come naturally. It never has, for you. I am far from perfect, but one thing I know for sure: as long as I'm in this world, my kids will always have someone in their corner. But... When Greg left me, and I was alone, watching the family I spent twenty-five years building just... collapse, where were you? Oh, right. You were in Europe, having sex. Chasing beauty. Do you think, if Mommy were here, she wouldn't have been by my side, camped out, picking me back up? Do you think I would have had to fly across the country just to remind her I was still alive?

So. Don't talk to me about love. Love is a word that still means something to me, and you don't know the first thing about it.

ELLIOT. You don't get to choose people's words, Jodi.

JODI. No, I don't. But I won't validate this with my presence.

ELLIOT. Then don't.

JODI. So you choose Trey over me?

ELLIOT. No. I'm not choosing anyone. You are invited to my table. In my house. You decide.

(He exits upstairs. **JODI** *sits for a beat.)*

*(***JEFF*** *enters and cleans up.* **JODI** *watches him.)*

JODI. I didn't realize you and my dad had all that history.

JEFF. Ancient history, now.

JODI. Well, it looked like a beautiful trip.

*(***JEFF*** *thinks back to the trip, fondly.)*

JEFF. It was. But. Anything that's very beautiful only lasts a very short time.

(He exits as **ELLIOT** *comes downstairs with* **TREY** *and* **BENJAMIN.** **ELLIOT** *exits to the dining room.* **TREY** *approaches* **JODI.***)*

JODI. Honestly? I'm sorry, but I can't.

TREY. You're gonna be my stepdaughter now.

(Beat.)

Dinner's inside, if you want –

JODI. I'm not. I...

TREY. We're having chicken.

(He exits.)

BENJAMIN. What happened?

JODI. Daddy *loves* Trey. He's gonna *marry* Trey. And we can either join their wedding feast, or not.

BENJAMIN. Well, next time don't make someone feel bad if they forget a gift.

JODI. Yeah no shit.

BENJAMIN. It's gonna be ok, Mom.

JODI. No, it's not. It's not ok honey.

And now your brother's been arrested for dealing drugs at school. To sixth-graders.

BENJAMIN. What?

JODI. Your brother. They think he's been dealing drugs. To sixth-graders.

BENJAMIN. WHAT? Oh my god, he – why didn't anyone tell me – I didn't know – Grayson was ARRESTED?

(Beat.)

JODI. No. I just wanted to see how it'd feel if things were going any worse.

BENJAMIN. Oh my god, Mom, don't do that.

JODI. Sorry.

(Beat.)

BENJAMIN. This family sucks.

JODI. Oh Benji, don't say that.

BENJAMIN. Why? It's true.

JODI. I know, but not every true thing has to be said aloud.

BENJAMIN. Maybe, but... you know what I realized? When Grandma Sylvia dies, there'll be no one left to call me faygele.

JODI. Good! That's called progress.

BENJAMIN. I guess, but for some reason I find it depressing.

JODI. Well, honey, that's because you're odd.

BENJAMIN. I know, but it still makes me sad.

(Quick beat.)

BENJAMIN. Let's get out of here. You wanna go to the Mercer?

JODI. I want room service.

BENJAMIN. In bed?

JODI. Room service, in bed, with the covers pulled up to my chin.

BENJAMIN. That sounds nice.

JODI. It sounds really nice.

BENJAMIN. Yeah, it does. Alright. Let's go pack.

> *(He rises, makes his way to the stairs, sees **JODI** hasn't moved.)*

Mom? Are you coming?

JODI. I don't know...

> *(A long beat, as **JODI** thinks, and **BENJAMIN** waits.)*
>
> *(Then **ELLIOT** enters, carrying a plate of chicken paillard, with a knife and fork.)*
>
> *(He sits beside **JODI** and begins to cut the chicken. He tries to offer it to her, but when she doesn't respond, he brings it to her mouth, almost as if he were feeding a small child. **JODI** turns her face away, rejecting the offer. Then she turns back, opens her mouth, and eats.)*
>
> *(The taste of this one bite floods her with memory. She takes her time chewing it.)*

ELLIOT. Good?

> *(**JODI** nods.)*
>
> *(Then **TREY** appears, carrying two more plates. He hands one to **ELLIOT**, brings the other to **BENJAMIN**.)*
>
> *(**ORSOLYA** appears right after and hands a plate to **TREY** as **JEFF** enters with water glasses.)*
>
> *(**BENJAMIN** sits in a chair. **TREY** sits on the floor and begins to eat.)*

(BENJAMIN watches JODI. JODI watches her father as he eats.)

(After a long beat, JODI picks up the knife and fork, cuts into the chicken, and takes a second bite.)

(We leave them here, knowing only that a family is trying to have dinner together.)

End of Play

Printed in the USA
CPSIA information can be obtained
at www.ICGtesting.com
LVHW010858091223
766044LV00019B/1557